Crashing Together

An Across the Hall Novella - Book 2

AJ Claremont

Let's Collective Publishing

www.ajclaremont.com

Edited by Alysha Thornton @athorntonedits
Cover Design: 100covers.com

First Edition: 2026

Contents

To Jen,

We are a waste of flesh, *and I wouldn't have it any other way*

Chapter 1

Liam

I always thought rock bottom would feel more dramatic. Turns out, it just smells like warm beer and regret.

"You don't have to go home, kid," Frankie says without looking up from where he's wiping down the bar. "But you can't stay here."

I didn't have a home to go home to. That's why I'd been at this dimly lit bar every night since Cal took off for Cambodia a week and a half ago. Or maybe it was Cancun, somewhere with palm trees and no cell service.

Most nights end the same: Frankie kicking me out, me stumbling back to Cal's apartment, collapsing face-first into his bed, and sleeping until either the woman across the hall screams into her phone on her way to work, or I have to piss badly enough to crawl out from under the covers.

Technically, I did have a home. I grew up twenty minutes from here. My mom still lives in the same house, still has my trophies on a shelf. But I hadn't told her I was back in town yet. I hadn't told anyone, aside from Cal, that the Iron Cats let me go and that my big league dreams had quietly died somewhere on a half-lit field in Reno. I sure as hell hadn't told my mom I was crashing at my best friend's apartment and drinking myself numb every night trying not to think about how badly I'd screwed it all up.

I toss two twenties on the bar, but Frankie comes over and slides the bills back toward me.

"I'll put your drinks on Cal's tab," he says, turning to re-shelve bottles before I can object. I put the bills back in my pocket because, let's be honest, I'm in no place to argue.

Minor league baseball players barely make minimum wage, so I'd made ends meet by doing the other players' taxes—I have a weird brain for numbers. I used to tell myself I'd pay off my mom's mortgage once I hit the big leagues, finally repay her for everything she gave up for me. But that dream was as flat as the last sip of beer in this bottle.

I let out a long sigh and figure I should head back to Cal's. I'm not really sure what to do with myself these days. My entire life, since I was fourteen, has revolved around baseball—grueling training, a perfect diet, and studying the game like my life depended on it. Because let's face it, every day you're trying to get called up feels like the most important test you'll ever take. I have zero hobbies, hardly any friends, and I barely even date. Scratch that—I don't date. I don't have time.

I push off the stool and head for the door when a brunette in a strappy tank top and denim skirt gives me that look—the one I know well. The one I've seen in countless bars and hotel lobbies across the US. I've been an athlete my whole life, and I have a face that apparently works in my favor. I might not have time for actual relationships, but I know that without much effort, I could take her home or find a dark corner here. I know my reputation, and honestly, most women seem to want exactly what I have time for—one night, no complications, usually that works for everyone involved.

But even that doesn't sound appealing right now.

Besides, once she finds out I'm just a washed-up ex minor leaguer with a pretty face and not her ticket to the WAG lifestyle, she probably won't want to waste her time anyway. Hell, I'm technically homeless right now. As soon as I was cut, I broke my lease on the apartment I could never really afford anyway. I packed the stuff I cared about into two duffel bags—both of which are still unpacked on Cal's living room floor—and left El Paso to come back to San Francisco.

I give her a tight nod and push through the bar doors to the chilly night. Now, here I was, on the sidewalk in front of Bar None, mooching off my childhood best friend's generosity and wallowing in self-pity. I need to figure out a job, a place to live, and what the fuck I'm doing with my life besides being a has-been ball player with a bruised ego and a mountain of debt.

But that's a problem for tomorrow.

By the time I reach Cal's front door, my vision is so blurry I can barely make out the keypad. But somehow, I manage to stumble into the darkened apartment, strip off my jeans and hoodie, toss them onto the bed, and then collapse face-first into it.

Pretty sure I pass out before my head even hits the pillow.

Chapter 2

Sophie

Cal: *Sophie, if you ever need a place to crash, you can always come to my place.*

I reread the three-month-old text from my brother and hope his offer still stands. Not that I could call to confirm, since he was off somewhere saving the world while my life was falling apart. Typical. I quickly wiped the tears forming in the corners of my eyes.

I shift the duffle bag full of everything I own higher on my shoulder and adjust my grip on the roll of canvases. My grandmother's old art supply box weighs down my other arm—my prized possession, even if it's been gathering dust for months. I start up the stairs, trying to be quiet so as not to disturb Cal's neighbors.

It has to be close to 3 a.m., but I couldn't sleep in my cramped house anymore. Not while my *boyfriend*—or, as he insisted on being called, my *emotional co-creator*—was fucking one of our roommates in the next room, possibly two of them. To be fair, he *had* invited me to join, but I'd told him a thousand times I wasn't into that. But according to him, "monogamy is a tool of capitalism," and my refusal was "a trauma response rooted in ownership culture." Also, I was apparently failing to honor his "universal desire to have his body worshiped by multiple lifeforms." I had my bags packed by the time he reached his "spiritual climax affirmation."

It's called a fucking orgasm, dude—not that he'd ever given me one.

So I drove the ninety minutes from Santa Cruz to San Francisco, circled for twenty minutes to find street parking, and lugged my entire life inside. By the time I hit the landing in front of Cal's apartment, my arms were burning, my heart was broken, and I had exactly zero regrets.

I punched in the door code—our mom's birthdate—and went inside.

It was pitch black, and my heart sank a little as I confirmed I was alone. But what had I expected? Cal was in Cambodia for twelve weeks, and I hadn't seen him in six months. Not since we met for dinner and he tried to talk me out of my current living and romantic situation, saying he was worried about me. What was new? Everyone had been telling me what to do since I was ten years old, and people figured out I could draw a little better than the average fifth grader.

I told Cal that he didn't need to worry, that I could make my own decisions. I was in love with Marshall and enjoyed communal living with a rotating door of roommates in a two-bedroom shithole cabin in the Santa Cruz mountains, and I wasn't attached to material things like he was. He just nodded and told me that if I ever changed my mind, his place was always available.

As I stand in his darkened apartment, I must admit that I *am* looking forward to enjoying some of his material things: consistent hot water, a dishwasher, and most of all, his king-sized bed with its ridiculously high thread count sheets.

I consider taking a shower, but suddenly I'm overwhelmed with fatigue. I think the rush of anger and adrenaline is draining from my body, and everything is catching up with me. I can barely keep my eyes open. I'll crash in Cal's bed tonight and sort everything else out in the morning.

I stumble into Cal's room and don't even have the energy to dig out my pajamas that I'd stuffed into my duffel. I strip down to my underwear and pull on Cal's hoodie, which he'd left at the end of his bed, and climb in.

I'm asleep before my head hits the pillow.

Chapter 3

Liam

I wake with my arm draped over the warm curve of her bare hip and her ass firmly in my lap. My dick responds as my hand wanders under her hoodie—my hoodie—and I squeeze her ample breast.

She lets out a little moan.

Somewhere in the back of my hungover, sleep haze, I try to remember if I brought that woman home from the bar last night. But she had short hair. My face is currently buried in a wild mess of curls that sprawl across my pillow. I squeeze her breast a little harder this time, needing to hear that throaty moan from her again.

Maybe this is a dream. A hot as fuck wet dream like I am a goddamned teenager, but I don't care. My dream girl wiggles her ass tighter against my erection, and I push my dick against her thin panties and pinch her nipple.

"Uh-huh," she whimpers. And I need to get my hand between her luscious thighs.

"Let me touch you, baby," I whisper in her curl-covered ear. "Let me make you come."

I slide my hand down over the swell of her belly and tease the top of her underwear. She rolls into me.

"Liam?"

"Yes, baby," I nuzzle into her neck and dip my finger into the elastic of her underwear. Until she shoves me off her...hard.

"What the fuck, Liam!" she screams and clambers away from me. It's still dark in Cal's bedroom, almost pitch black, and I think I'm still drunk because I can't remember what happened last night. But fuck, do I want to remember, I hope I worshiped every one of those juicy curves last night. I hope I feasted between those thighs.

"What...where did...what the hell?" she stammers before flipping on the light.

I throw my hands over my eyes from the painful onslaught of light when a pillow is launched at my head. "I'm serious, Liam Blake. What are you doing here?"

"What's happening?" I mutter, pulling my hands away from my face, my eyes adjusting enough to see the gorgeous woman now standing in her underwear and my Iron Cats hoodie at the foot of the bed.

My still-drunk brain finally catches up. She's older now, with grown-up curves, soft angles, and full lips. I barely recognize her. But she still has the same wild curls she had as a kid and the same baby blue eyes, just like Cal's.

Realization dawns on me like a cold shower I didn't sign up for.

I was about to finger my best friend's little sister.

Chapter 4
Sophie

My crush on Liam Blake started the first day my brother brought him home for dinner when I was ten years old. And I didn't understand why one of my stupid brother's stupid friends made my tummy feel weird.

They were the only two freshmen on the varsity baseball team—Cal made it because he was tall, and Liam because he was a better baseball player at fourteen than most of the seniors. Back then, Liam had a mop of dirty blonde hair, a smattering of freckles across his nose, and he called my mom "ma'am."

But now Liam Blake is lying in my brother's bed, naked except for a very small pair of black boxer briefs that do absolutely nothing to hide his enormous erection. His chest is broad and tanned, his thighs thick with muscle. He has the same messy hair and freckles he had as a teen. As I stare at him, trying to make sense of what the hell is happening, I realize he still makes my tummy feel weird.

"Soph?" Liam says, blinking and climbing out of the bed. "What are you doing here?" His voice is soft and filled with concern. He reaches a hand across the bed to me, and a strange part of me wants to go to him, to have him pull me against that sturdy chest and tell me everything is going to be okay.

"What the hell are *you* doing here?!?" I shout instead. "And can you put on some fucking pants?" I cross my arms over my chest and attempt to tear my eyes away from his body, but fail miserably. I can't stop staring.

"Sophie, I'm so sorry," Liam says, fumbling with his jeans. "I didn't know you were...it was...I didn't mean to," he tries to get out. I can't help but notice he's having trouble buttoning his jeans. Suddenly, my mouth goes a little dry.

"Why are you here, Liam?" I ask again, not making eye contact.

"Cal's letting me stay here while he's on assignment," Liam says. "He didn't tell me you were coming."

"Yeah, well," I wrap my arms around my body a little tighter, "I didn't tell him I was coming." My voice tips up a little at the end, and I swallow before my eyes can fill with tears.

"Are you okay?" Liam asks, and there is so much care in his three little words.

"Yeah," I steel myself, "My living situation just got a little...crowded. Cal told me if I ever needed a place to stay, I could come here."

"Of course," Liam nods, "I'll get my stuff packed up."

"And leave?" I ask, suddenly not wanting that to be the case.

"Um, well, it's four am," Liam says, biting his bottom lip and looking around. "Maybe I could chill on the couch until the sun comes up, and then I'll get out of your hair?"

"Were you going to stay here the whole time Cal's away?"

"Yeah, I'm kinda...between things right now." Liam stuffs his hands into his jeans pockets, a lock of hair falling over his downcast eyes. I think about the house in Santa Cruz—and Marshall's delusional, pretentious, faux-spiritual justification for why I should be okay with him sleeping around—and I know I'm never going back there. So I guess I'm kind of between things right now, too.

I go into Cal's walk-in closet and come out with a stack of blankets and an extra pillow. I hold them out to Liam.

"Okay, well, we'll figure it out in the morning."

Liam nods and takes the stack from me. Our fingers brush, and I remember the way his hands wandered all over my body just moments before. The way he squeezed my boobs just this side of painful, and how he whispered that he wanted to make me come. My whole body shudders, and I hope it's still too dark for Liam to see. "See you in the morning."

Liam nods again and turns to the bedroom door. Just before he leaves the room, he turns back around and smiles a lazy half-smile that instantly makes heat pool in my core.

"Nice sweatshirt, Soph," he says and walks out, closing the door behind him.

I look down at the oversized Iron Cats hoodie—the minor league team he plays for. I've been following his career for years. He'd made the All-Star team in his first year in the minors and led the league in on-base percentage for two consecutive seasons. I wonder why he's crashing at Cal's in the middle of the season?

I tuck my nose into the neck of his sweatshirt. It smells a bit like beer, but mostly like the musky, spicy scent I'd woken up wrapped in. I should probably change now that I know it's not my brother's sweatshirt.

I glance at the bedroom door before crawling into bed and turning off the light.

Chapter 5

Liam

I didn't actually touch her.

Not on purpose anyway. I'm lying on the couch in the dark, staring at the ceiling and having an imaginary conversation with my best friend, trying to explain why I'd fondled his baby sister.

Except I did touch her—roughly. And she liked it. I'd been with enough women to know she liked it. And I was about to put my hands in her underwear, *but I swear, Cal,* I didn't realize it was Sophie.

And I didn't know she'd grown up and filled out that lanky preteen body. I didn't know she had exceptional breasts and skin that felt like velvet under my fingers. I didn't know she smelled like vanilla and blueberries and a lot like me, all wrapped up in the sweatshirt I'd been wearing for days on end. I didn't know how much I would enjoy seeing her in that sweatshirt and underwear so thin I could see the outline of her blonde curls beneath them.

Fuck. Now I had another boner on my best friend's couch, thinking about how hot his sister is. The little girl who used to follow us around with a sketchpad and ask stupid questions about baseball stats.

That little girl who is now a gorgeous woman right behind that bedroom door. I wonder if she's still wearing my hoodie.

And if she isn't, what is she wearing? Her duffle bag is on the floor out here, so she's either wearing my clothes...or she's naked.

My dick bounces at that thought.

Or she's wearing her brother's clothes, my inner voice tries to remind me. *Your best friend, the one who you would be homeless without his generosity right now. Get your dick and head in the game, Blake.*

Besides, Sophie doesn't want me. As soon as she realized it was me touching her, she pushed away like I had the fucking plague. She threw a pillow at my head and told me to put my pants on. She clearly was not happy to wake up and find me fondling her breasts.

Her perfect, way-more-than-a-handful breasts. I wanted to see how much of those breasts I could fit in my mouth.

I had to do something more productive than talk to myself and lust after my accidental roommate, who was barely...how old would she be now? I was thirty-one, and she was in middle school during my senior year, so she was, what, five years younger than me? So, twenty-six? Twenty-six wasn't bad. I'd been with girls her age.

Liam Fucking Blake. Do a hundred push-ups right now, you pervert.

I roll off the couch and yank on my t-shirt, the cotton clinging to skin still damp with sweat. I drop to the floor and grind out a hundred push-ups, anything to burn off this energy sparking through my body.

Then, a hundred sit-ups.

Then, a hundred squats.

My muscles scream, and I think about doing burpees to punish myself. But it's barely 5 a.m., and the last thing I want to do is wake the neighbors.

Or worse—wake Sophie.

She looked like she needed sleep last night. When she finally turned on the light, she was beautiful, but I could see the red rimming of tears in her eyes. Showing up at your brother's apartment in the middle of the night rarely meant someone was in a good place.

I walk into the kitchen, wiping the sweat off my brow with the hem of my t-shirt. My head is pounding with day five of a hangover, and my muscles are shaking after my little torture session.

I fill a glass at the sink and down the whole thing. Then I take the Advil bottle out of the cabinet and shake two into my hand, refilling the glass.

"Can I have a couple of those, too?" Sophie asks, emerging from Cal's bedroom, startling me. She's pulled her wild curls back away from her face, and she's wearing a faded Lowell High sweatshirt of Cal's and a pair of his basketball shorts that are so big she has them rolled at least four times at the waist, making them hit her about mid-thigh.

I liked her 4 a.m. outfit better, but I nod and shake two pills into her outstretched hand. She reaches for my water with her other hand, and I pass it to her. Honestly, I'm about two seconds from handing over my wallet and keys, too.

She pops the pills into her mouth and throws back her head. I watch the line of her throat as she swallows.

"Is the Advil for your knee?" she asks.

"It's for my raging hangover," I say as she rounds the island and stops in front of me, giving me a once-over before hopping up onto the counter.

"Why are you here and not in El Paso?" she asks.

"I'm taking a break," I reply. "Why are you here and not in art school?"

"I'm taking a break," she fires back. "You don't just take a break in the middle of the season, Liam. Unless you're injured or benched. You haven't missed a game in three years."

She knows I haven't missed a game in three years? Well, what did it matter? What did any of it matter now? All the work, all the hours in the gym and the batting cages, all the sacrifices—it didn't matter now. I turn away from Sophie's gaze, afraid she'll notice the sting behind my eyes before I can blink it back.

"Cal said you have some douchebag boyfriend. Is that why you're here?" I try to change the subject from my failed athletic career.

"Cal called him a douchebag?"

"No," I laugh and shake my head. "He said he was a pseudo-intellectual performance piece with a man bun who wasn't good enough for you. I called him a douchebag."

"He is kind of a douchebag," she says with a mirthless laugh.

"What kind of douchebag? He didn't hurt you, did he, Soph?" My hand is already closing into a fist.

"No," she shook her head, but I wasn't so sure. "But I'm not going back there."

"I get it," I say, pushing off the counter. "I'll get packed up and head out."

"No—wait!" she calls out. I turn just as she hops off the counter and follows me into the living room. "I mean...we both need a place to stay, right? And Cal always said his door was open. If you don't mind the couch, maybe we can just...coexist? At least until one of us figures something else out."

She flashes me a small smile. An errant curl has fallen across her cheek, and I have the undeniable urge to tuck it behind her ear.

This is a bad idea.

Cal would definitely not be thrilled about me shacking up with his little sister—especially not with the kind of thoughts I've been having about her. He's always been overprotective of her. Lately, however, bad ideas have been my specialty. And it's not like I have a ton of options. I'm not ready to crawl back to my mom's place, and I can't afford, well, anything else right now. I just need a few days to get my shit together. I can handle a few days with Sophie. Keep my dick in my pants and my thoughts to myself. It's not like she's interested anyway. I'm sure we can "coexist" like she said.

"I'm cool with the couch."

Chapter 6
Sophie

I didn't realize being cool with the couch meant becoming one with it, I think, as I step over three pairs of Liam's sneakers scattered by the bathroom door.

We've been "coexisting" for a week now, and as far as I can tell, he hasn't left that couch—except for his daily runs that happen at the crack of dawn and his brutal calisthenics sessions that turn the living room into his personal gym.

"Hey," he says, glancing up, then back at the TV. His feet are propped on one arm of the couch, and his head rests on the other. I can't understand how he's sleeping on that thing—he's easily a foot too tall.

"Shoot," I mutter, drumming my fingers against the counter as I try to remember what I'm forgetting. Laptop. I duck back into Cal's room.

When money got tight a few months ago, I answered an ad for a "freelance content assistant." Which basically means I write fake reviews for Etsy ebooks and overly enthusiastic comments on TikToks I've never watched. It's soul-sucking, but it pays. Just not enough. Not having to pay rent for a couple of months while I'm at Cal's will help, but with student loan payments and future rent, I'll need to find something more stable, and soon.

Liam's flipping through channels on Cal's massive TV, not really watching anything. A beer dangles from his hand, another already empty on the coffee table. I'm in no position to judge since I'm just emerging from bed at 1 p.m. Cal's apartment is open concept—the kitchen and living room blend into one big space with hardly any privacy. Which is why I've spent the last three days holed up in Cal's room, rotating between naps and smutty romance novels.

I may or may not be rereading the one about the bad boy MLB player and the no-nonsense publicist hired to clean up his image. Last night, I hit the locker room scene—the one with the publicist, the player, and some very creative finger work, and my imagination may have wandered...along with my hand.

I shake the thought from my head. I need to get it together and not be lusting after my accidental roommate, who has been keeping his obvious distance in the last five days.

"So," I manage, my voice still a little higher than I'd like. "Good day?" I pluck a sweaty t-shirt off the back of the barstool.

"Yup." He takes a long pull from his beer, eyes flicking to the shirt dangling from my fingers. "Just toss it on the pile. I'll get to laundry later."

I toss it in the pile and set my laptop on the counter—completely dead. I sigh and scan the room.

"It's next to the armchair," Liam says, not even glancing away from the TV.

Sure enough, my charger is plugged in there. "Thanks," I mumble.

"It's freezing in here," I mutter as a gust of cold air hits me. I walk over to the wide-open window. "Did you forget you're in San Francisco, not El Paso?"

Without warning, he pulls his shirt over his head. My brain short-circuits. His chest is broad, the line of his shoulder looks sculpted from marble, and I can count every single defined ab muscle. There's a trail of dark hair that disappears into the waistband of his sweatpants. When he twists to toss his shirt onto the growing laundry heap, the cords of his forearms pop, and I nearly forget how windows work.

"You can close it," he says, catching my stare. "Sorry, I run a little hot."

Boy, does he ever.

I slam the window shut with a little more force than necessary and zip my hoodie up to my chin. "It's fine," I mutter. "Let's just try to keep Karl the Fog outside."

I pull a cereal box off the kitchen shelf and stuff a handful into my mouth while waiting for my computer to come back to life. I get started on my latest series of "Oh, this book changed my life" posts, shaking Froot Loops directly into my mouth for every heartfelt review I fake.

"You don't really eat, do you?" Liam asks from his residence on the couch, and I look down at the box in my hand.

"I think the fact that I'm actively putting food in my mouth means I eat."

"I just mean I haven't seen you eat an actual meal since we've been here," he says, swinging himself off the couch. He's not wrong. I don't really cook. I get distracted easily, so I graze all day long—cereal, cheese sticks, PB&J if I really want to make an effort.

He walks into the kitchen, still shirtless, all lean muscle and that infuriating V of his abs that acts like a neon arrow pointing straight to the waistband of his now dangerously low-slung sweats. I take a few self-preserving steps back as he rounds the counter and pulls open the fridge.

"Do you like salmon?" Liam asks, pulling out a glass storage container.

I nod and try to swallow the lump in my throat. He opens the pantry door and takes out two microwavable rice packets.

"Have you heard of the viral salmon bowls?" he asks, gesturing to the bowls on the open shelf above my head.

"I make a living scrolling TikTok, so yes, I've heard of them," I reply, handing him the bowls.

"I thought you made a living doing art?" he asks, taking condiments out of the fridge.

"Art is...complicated." He glances over the fridge door like he's going to say something. "Kinda like baseball."

"Got it," he says and shuts the fridge.

Less than ten minutes later, we're sitting side by side at the breakfast bar, eating the most delicious salmon bowls—the ones that went viral a few years ago but always felt too complicated for me to attempt. Liam threw this lunch together with stuff I didn't even realize we had in the house.

After we eat, I clean the dishes, then stress-clean the entire kitchen. When my life feels chaotic, scrubbing counters calms me down. Liam offers to help, but I wave him off, insisting that since he cooked, the least I can do is clean.

"I'd hardly call that cooking," he says, but he gives me my space as he grabs his own laptop and settles back on the couch. "That was more like microwaving."

I start the dishwasher and put away all the ingredients from our lunch. While I clean, I steal glances at Liam, tapping away on his computer. Sometimes his face is scrunched in concentration, and sometimes I catch him watching me before we both quickly look away.

"What are you working on?" I ask, opening my laptop again after the kitchen is gleaming to my liking.

"I do the taxes for a couple of the guys on the Iron Cats," he says. "We don't make a lot of money in the minors, so pretty much everyone has side jobs."

"You do their taxes?"

"Yeah, Soph," he chuckles. "That's my side job."

I know he doesn't make a big league salary yet, but he's doing other guys' taxes? He also hasn't told me why he's taking a break from baseball, but this is the first conversation in the past week that's been longer than me asking, "Is this your sweaty shirt?" and him complaining, "Can we please open a goddamn window? It's a hundred degrees in here." I also haven't told him why all my art supplies are still in a heap next to the front door, exactly where I dropped them at 3 a.m. that first night.

That first night. When Liam slid his hands into my panties and asked if he could make me come.

"You okay?" Liam asks, and I realize I closed my eyes and might have been biting my bottom lip.

"Yup, totally!" I squeak, "Well, we should both get some work done!"

We both work in companionable silence for the rest of the afternoon. True to his word, Liam eventually takes a break, scoops up all his laundry scattered around the house, and starts a load. I don't say anything when he cracks the window again.

"Thanks again for taking the couch," I say later, when Liam is making up his bed.

"Sure," he says, fluffing his pillow. "It makes sense, I'm kinda an early-to-bed, early-to-rise person. I blame it on two decades of early morning practices."

His forearms flex as he tucks the blanket into the couch cushions, the definition in his quads visible through the tight pull of his shorts. I suck in a small inhale.

"Sorry," he says, turning towards me when I realize I haven't responded to him. "Do I wake you up in the mornings? I try to be quiet."

"No," I shake my head and try to regain my composure. "Living with five people teaches you how to sleep through—" I pause, thinking of Marshall's orgasm chant the night I left, "—pretty much anything."

A few beats of quiet pass between us.

"Okay then," I say, turning towards Cal's room. "I'll let you get to bed."

"Night, Soph. See you in the morning."

And for reasons I don't fully understand yet, I'm actually looking forward to that.

Chapter 7

Liam

Sophie emerges from Cal's room, all sleep rumpled and wild curls, and walks straight to his overcomplicated espresso machine, which I still haven't figured out. She carries two perfect lattes into the living room, silently placing one on the coffee table in front of me, then settling into the chair, tucking her legs underneath her, and taking a long sip. Her eyes close, and I watch the way her chest rises and falls with her breathing.

Over the past week, we've fallen into this weird little rhythm. I make sure she eats something that doesn't come from a box, and she makes sure we don't die of dysentery—I swear she scrubs the counters within an inch of their lives every day. I keep track of where she drops her keys and her phone charger. And every morning, she makes me the perfect caffeinated shot without a word, like it's no big deal. But I kind of think it is.

She opens her eyes, and I quickly avert mine, back to my laptop. She looks around the table. "Do you see my—"

I hold up her ridiculous pink pen that she tucks into her messy bun, but it always falls out when she leans over.

"Thanks," she says.

I'm still dying to ask her about her art. As a kid, she was always drawing or painting—not just the typical kid stuff.

She created full-blown masterpieces and sophisticated concepts when she was barely fourteen. After Cal and I went off to college, Cal told me that she had gotten into a private art high school and had her first solo gallery exhibit before graduating. However, her pile of art supplies hadn't moved since she arrived. I didn't understand this 'content assistant' thing she was doing, which didn't seem related to art, but I didn't ask. After all, I hadn't exactly been open about being dumped from the Iron Cats, so I guess neither of us was ready to talk about what was really going on.

Whatever this domestic routine was, it was temporary. Convenient. Two people crashing at the same place. Nothing more.

"We're pathetic," Sophie says, standing up after we've both been rotting on the couch, hands on her hips like she's gearing up for a full-blown intervention. "We need to put on real pants and leave the house."

I glance up, caught somewhere between amused and intrigued. "Yeah? Got somewhere in mind?"

She shrugs, but there's a spark in her eyes that's new. "Let's walk down to that bar on the corner. One drink. Pretend we're real people."

The thought shouldn't excite me this much, but it does. Not just the chance to get out—but getting out with her. "Alright," I say, pushing upright. "But I need a shower first."

"Same," she says, cringing a little. "I honestly can't remember the last time I showered."

"Probably another sign we need to leave the house," I reply, trying not to picture her in the shower—but now it's all I can think about. And because there's no way I'm standing up now without making things weird, I add, "You go first."

"Welcome back, kid," Frankie says as Sophie and I enter Bar None. "I wondered if you'd ended up in a ditch after the last time I kicked you out."

My eyes dart to Sophie, but she seems unbothered by Frankie's assessment. The truth is, after spending hours a night here the first week I was in town, I hadn't been back in the two weeks since Sophie showed up. "Good to see you too, Frankie," I say and don't elaborate.

"Your usual?" Frankie asks.

"You have a usual at this bar?" Sophie asks, but it's more of a tease than a judgment.

"I mean, it's just a beer," I say, then add, "And a shot of tequila." *Then repeat until I pass out in Cal's bed,* I think, and I feel a little embarrassed by past Liam's drinking behavior.

"Make it two," Sophie says to Frankie.

Frankie sets our drinks on the bar. Sophie passes me a tequila shot before picking up her own. "To leaving the house," she toasts, and we clink our glasses. I watch the creamy column of her neck as she tips back to shoot the drink. Her curls spill down her back, and her cheeks flush when the alcohol hits her tongue. My mouth goes dry.

"What?" she asks, setting the empty glass down on the bar and sucking the lime between her teeth.

"Nothing," I say quickly and take my shot.

"Liam!" a woman calls from the back corner of the bar. Cal's downstairs neighbor, whom I'd met before he left.

"Is that Liv?" Sophie asks, waving back. She grabs her beer and heads towards the booth where Liv is sitting with her eccentric roommate and some other guy.

"Sophie?" Liv stands as we approach the table, pulling Sophie into a hug. "What are you doing here?"

"Oh," Sophie says. "Cal said I could stay at his place any time I needed, so...I'm crashing there while he's away."

"I thought you were crashing there?" Liv turns towards me, and my insides tighten.

"Liam and I go way back," Sophie explains before I can answer. "He's like another brother. We're coexisting."

I can't explain why Sophie's assessment stings. It's one thing for me to remind myself we're just coexisting—it's another thing to hear her dismiss us so casually to someone else. We are just coexisting. I'm sleeping on the couch, and we just circle each other all day. So she's not wrong, but do I want her to be?

"Yeah, it's cool," I say.

"You two want to join us?" Liv asks, and as she gestures toward her companions in the big round booth. "You remember my roommate Andy?"

The perky blonde waves from the booth. "Hey."

"And this is Owen, my fiancé." Liv gazes at him with hearts in her eyes. "I can't believe I get to say that for real now."

My eyes snag on the guy—the same one I met in Cal's lobby, the so-called fake boyfriend. Except judging by the way he's glued to Liv—and the rock on her finger—there's nothing fake about it. Sure, I've spent most of the past few weeks drunk or hungover, but I'm sure it was only three weeks ago I was giving her some pathetic baseball-as-love pep talk. Guess it worked.

"You're engaged?" Sophie asks, grabbing her hand and inspecting the ring.

"We kind of did things a little backward," Owen says sheepishly, holding out his hand to shake mine. "Good to see you again, Liam."

"Perfect for us," Liv corrects. "Pretending to be engaged was exactly what we needed to figure out we wanted it to be real."

"Yeah, I have to listen to how *real* it is every night," Andy says, making a gesture with her hands I haven't seen since middle school, but everyone else seems to be used to her antics and ignores her.

Before I can suggest we find our own table, Sophie settles in by Liv. Leaving me to take the seat next to Andy, who greets me with a wink.

"I met Sophie," Liv explains to Owen, "when Cal invited Andy and me to her gallery exhibition here in the City, what? Almost three years ago?"

Sophie nods, tight-lipped.

"Three years ago?" Owen asks. "That's impressive for someone so young."

"That wasn't even her first one," Andy supplies. "Sophie is an art prodigy."

"Cal likes to blow things out of proportion." Sophie takes a casual sip of her beer, but I'm confused. Sophie *is* an art prodigy. She was taking college-level art classes in middle school, and her parents had a framed ink drawing of hers that looked like a photograph—one she'd done when she was six. Even if she hasn't painted in a while, that doesn't change her skill.

"What kind of art?" Owen asks, taking a sip of his own drink.

"Large-scale abstracts as a visual interpretation of emotional memory," Sophie answers, but her voice has lost all its warmth. She sounds like a robot repeating a well-rehearsed speech.

"Huh," Owen muses, "Sounds interesting."

No, it sounds like bullshit. Sophie is so much more than a cliché academic stereotype.

Liv swipes through her phone before handing it over to Owen. "This is her work."

Sophie's eyes flick towards the door like she wants to escape. I try to catch her eye to let her know I'm ready to bolt with her if she gives the word.

"Wow, these are really striking," Owen says, scrolling through the photos. He looks up at Sophie. "I might know someone who'd be interested in commissioning something like this—my client, Senator Langford, is furnishing her DC apartment."

Sophie shifts in her seat. "I mean, I'm not really...I haven't been taking on new work lately." She takes a sip of her beer.

"Just thought I'd mention it," Owen says. "She's got great taste and a good budget for the right piece."

Sophie nods noncommittally. "Yeah, maybe. We'll see."

Her posture shifts, slumping forward a little, as she picks at the label of her beer. The light in her eyes has dimmed. Owen scrolls through the photos on Liv's phone, tossing out comments about his client's taste for high-end abstract art. I don't know why his praise rattles her, but I want to reach across the table and reassure her. Instead, I fist my hands in my lap.

"How is your brother?" Liv asks, seemingly not noticing Sophie's shift in demeanor. "Have either of you heard from him since he left?"

Cal still doesn't know Sophie is living in his apartment, much less with me, and I'm not sure how he'll react when he finds out. Or maybe I do.

"Oh, you know Cal," Sophie says with a shrug. "Radio silence for weeks, then suddenly he'll FaceTime, and you better be available. Everything's on his terms."

"Older siblings," Liv laughs. "We've got them too," she gestures between her and Owen. "Same controlling energy, just without the humanitarian mission. What about you, Liam?"

"Just me," I say, tipping my beer. "My mom said I was all she could handle. That's why I practically lived at Cal and Sophie's growing up."

"Cal mentioned you're a big-time ballplayer?" Owen says.

Sophie's eyes snap to mine. "Liam was a high school All-American, and no one's beaten his home run record at our high school to this day," she starts, not looking away. "He played varsity all four years, got recruited by a bunch of top

D1 programs, he hit over .300 in college, and got drafted after his junior year—third round. And he can still gun a runner out at home from the outfield."

I can hardly swallow. I won't lie, listening to Sophie list off my stats makes my dick hard, but it also makes my insides flip a little, and that's a feeling I'm less accustomed to.

Sophie finally breaks our gaze, turning to Owen. "So, yeah, he's a ballplayer, not an exaggeration."

"Clearly," Owen nods. "You still play?"

I open my mouth with the same answer I'd been using for weeks—I'm taking a break—but the words die on my tongue.

But something about the way Sophie looked so deflated—like the fact that she was a little uncertain, suddenly changed her value—made me want to tell the truth.

"Actually, I was just cut," I say, and Sophie's breath catches. "My agent says there's still a shot I could get picked up mid-season if a roster spot opens up. But I'm thirty-one, I've got a nagging knee injury, and I'm too much of a risk for teams to take seriously anymore."

I shrug and take a long sip of my beer. Out of my periphery, Sophie's hand opens and closes, almost as if she wants to reach for me. An uncomfortable silence settles over the table. I didn't mean to drag down the mood, just to tell Sophie that whatever she was going through was okay.

"What about you, Andy?" I say, trying to change the subject. "Any siblings getting in your business?"

"Probably," she says, popping the pineapple chunk from her very pink beverage into her mouth.

"Probably?" Sophie asks, eyebrow lifted.

"Andy had a less-than-traditional upbringing," Liv explains, smiling.

"My parents are part of a traveling performance troupe," Andy says. "I grew up on the road, and I can still walk on stilts."

"What?" Sophie asks, laughing. "What kind of traveling performance troupe?"

"Count Voltaire's Cirque des Merveilles." Andy drags her hands through the air like she's illuminating the marquee.

"Like a traveling circus?" I ask, and Andy nods.

"But how does growing up in a circus relate to siblings?" Owen asks, and I admit, we are all hanging on her explanation.

"I think this conversation is going to require another round of drinks." Liv chuckles. "I'll grab refills."

Sophie stands to let Liv out, and I can't help but notice her gaze flick to the sliver of space next to me, like she'd like to move to my side of the booth. And, damn, I want her to. I want to feel her body next to mine, to tuck her close. But she changes her mind and sits back down.

"My parents think their partnership was created on a higher plane," Andy begins. "They're deeply in love but also consensually non-monogamous. They believe sex and love are separate experiences. My mom had other partners in the troupe—like Marv the illusionist. If I couldn't find her in our RV, she was in his. My dad, though, liked the townies. He'd go out with the other musicians on our last night in each town and disappear until sunrise, stumbling back just as the caravan pulled out. A few times, my mom had to pull over and scoop him up from the roadside. They'd kiss hello, and we'd roll on to the next town. So while I don't know of any siblings, I'm pretty sure there's a mini Edward Vale in Albuquerque or Des Moines or somewhere."

Liv returns to the table, expertly balancing five shot glasses between her fingers. She sets them down on the table and holds one up. Everyone else grabs a glass.

"To siblings!"

Chapter 8
Sophie

"I think this is the first time I haven't gotten kicked out of that bar," Liam says as we step onto the sidewalk in front of Bar None just after midnight.

"I feel like you have some stories to share," I say with a little hiccup. The night had been delightful. I was out of the house and actually talking to Liam, and I don't think I realized how much I was craving both. When Liv, Andy, and Owen said goodnight, I wasn't ready to head back to Cal's. So I suggested we stay for another drink. Honestly, I have no idea what my nightly total was, but it was way more than I was used to.

"Let's just say I didn't handle myself very responsibly when Cal first left," Liam explains.

"Why didn't you tell me you got cut?"

Liam drags his hand through his hair. "I don't know, maybe I haven't come to terms with it myself. That the career I've wanted since I was twelve is over, and I have nothing to show for it and no fucking clue what comes next."

"Welcome to the club," I say, stealing a glance at Liam's profile as we pass under a streetlight. The sharp angle of his jaw, the rise of his cheekbones, but also the sadness in his eyes. "But you said your agent still thinks there's a chance of getting picked up by another team."

"Yeah, but Soph," Liam shoves his hand into his jeans pocket, making his bicep bulge. "It's July. The chances of someone picking up a thirty-one-year-old with a bum knee this late in the season? Pretty damn low."

"Pretty damn low is not none," I tell him.

"And what do you mean by 'welcome to the club?' I'm pretty sure you just got a commissioned art piece out of tonight. Senator Langford? That's a huge deal, Soph."

"I doubt anything will come of it. No one at that table was exactly sober tonight. I'm sure Owen won't even remember to tell her about my art." I look down at a cigarette butt on the sidewalk. "Besides, she's not going to want a piece from some art school dropout."

Liam stops walking. "You dropped out of art school?"

"I figured Cal already told you." I shrug.

"He said you were taking a break. What's your version?"

I rarely talk about this, and I'm an expert at changing the subject. But maybe it's the tequila, or perhaps the way his eyes glint when he looks at me makes me want to tell him.

"When I was a kid, I loved to draw."

"I remember. You were never without your sketchbook."

I smile, surprised that too-cool-for-school Liam Blake ever noticed his friend's bratty little sister, much less her sketchbook.

"Other people realized I was talented, and it just snowballed," I say, and start walking again, thinking this will be easier if I don't have to look him in the eye. "One show led to another, and suddenly everyone wanted something—my art, a promise of future success, a piece of me. I never felt like I could stop and catch my breath. My parents were so proud, and I wanted to make them proud, but I think I just piled all this pressure on myself and on what my art was supposed to be. I'm not sure I was ever capable of living up to it."

"You're clearly capable of it, if Owen could tell from a blurry iPhone photo that Meredith Langford would be into your style."

"But that photo was taken three years ago. It's gotten harder and harder to live up to the expectations others had of me. Or maybe harder to live up to my own expectations."

"Welcome to the club," Liam echoes back, holding the front door to the apartment complex open for me.

I glance back as we climb the stairs and catch him looking at me. Really looking. His smile has faded, replaced by something heavier. Something that makes my pulse stutter. I hurry up the remaining steps, trying to keep from tripping.

I fumble with the keypad on Cal's door, the numbers swimming. "That might have been one too many tequilas," I mutter. "Or four."

Liam chuckles, low and warm. "Want me to try?"

I shift to the side, and although it's dim in the hallway, I can see the faint stubble that has appeared across his jaw. I want to trace it with my finger. He swallows, his Adam's apple bobbing before his eyes drop to my mouth, just for a flash, and I feel it everywhere.

I think about that first night when I climbed into bed with him. The way his hands felt on my waist, the way he pressed me close, the heat of him behind me, steady and solid.

I lean in, just a little. My hand brushes his chest, and I swear I can feel his pulse dancing under my palm. His fingers lift to my hair, threading in gently, sending a curl of heat to my core. His pupils are blown wide, and he's leaning in too now. He pauses on a ragged inhale, like he's giving me time to change my mind—but I don't want to. Not even a little.

His big palm cups the back of my head, angling me toward him, and my eyes flutter closed.

"I know it's late, Jessica, but the quarterly metrics don't sleep!" A voice shouts from the stairs.

We both jerk apart like we've been caught stealing.

Harper, Cal's neighbor, crests the final step, AirPod in her ear, heels in her hand, and a look of sheer disgust on her face. She barely glances at us, still whisper-shouting into her phone. "Tell Spencer sleep is for people who have met their KPIs."

I try the lock code one more time, and the door finally beeps. I push open the door and step inside without looking back at Liam.

Chapter 9
Liam

"I want to die," Sophie moans from the couch. "First, I want to have my stomach pumped, then I want to die."

I give her a glass of ice water and a cold washcloth before plopping down on the couch next to her.

"Ugh...too much movement," she groans, placing the cloth across her forehead. "I'm going to be carsick. Can you get carsick on a couch? And why is it so bright in here?"

It was nearly noon, and she'd just emerged from Cal's room. I was relieved she'd gotten a little sleep after the night she'd had. Around 4 a.m., I woke on the couch to the sound of her getting sick in the bathroom. I hated the thought of her being alone. I knocked gently, asked if she was okay—and when she didn't turn me away, I stepped in and held her hair back while her body purged the mess of our questionable drinking decisions.

"Drink that water," I tell her, pressing on my temples. I had been drinking too much since I turned sixteen. Why did last night's drinking have my head pounding like someone was trying to get out? "How much did we drink last night?"

"I lost count at seven," she says, her head rolling onto the back of the couch.

"Seven is a lot for a little pipsqueak like you," I say.

"I'm hardly a pipsqueak," she says dryly.

"I didn't mean anything,"

"Sorry, it's just that Marshall always told me I was too heavy for the waif aesthetic and not curvy enough to be a voluptuous ingénue."

My head snaps towards hers, and thank god her eyes are still closed—she doesn't see the way my gaze rakes over her body. Over those perfect curves, the dip of her tiny waist. The way she's stretched out on the couch makes her tank ride up, exposing toned abs, and her breasts strain against the fabric, barely contained. My dick responds instantly.

"I think your ex doesn't know what the hell he's talking about," I bite out.

Her head rolls to the side, like she can't bear to lift it, and she opens her eyes. A soft, almost wounded smile crosses her face.

"I think he thought he was helping, you know? He told me if I wanted to be taken seriously as an artist, I had to look the part."

"What the fuck does an artist look like?" And maybe it's a good thing my head is still throbbing, and I am in no condition to drive, because I'm about to pay a visit to Mr. Artsy McDouchebag.

Sophie rests her hand on my knee, and warmth blooms in my chest. "Liam, it's okay," she soothes. Her thumb traces a small circle on my jeans, and I wonder if she's even aware of what she's doing. "I haven't painted in months, so there is no part to look like."

"I'm not sure you can stop being an artist," I say. "You might not be making art at the moment, but I think being an artist is in your bones—like me being a baseball player."

She nods, but I can tell she's not convinced.

"Besides, what about this commission?"

"Liam, please." She holds up her hand, and I miss its warmth on my leg. "Senator Langford isn't going to call me. Drunk people's ideas don't always make sense sober."

I almost kissed her last night. Would that apply to her "drunk people ideas?" Because I'm sobering up, and it somehow still makes sense.

We spend the rest of the day sprawled out on various pieces of living room furniture. We eat saltines and drink ginger ale. Sophie naps on the couch, letting out soft puffing breaths and mumbling every so often. I flick on the TV so I don't keep watching her like a total weirdo.

When she wakes, we find a *Survivor* rerun marathon and settle in to armchair quarterback. Sophie starts at the far end of the couch, but with each episode, she drifts closer, until by the fifth episode she's curled against my side, her bare legs folded beneath her. I force myself to focus on the TV instead of the smooth skin of her thighs.

"I need a shower," Sophie declares, but doesn't move from the nest she's made next to me. "There's probably vomit in my hair."

"Sorry, that was my fault."

"No, you kept it from being a lot of vomit." She covers her face with her hands. "I can't believe you held my hair while I puked. That is way beyond the roommate code of conduct."

"I didn't mind," I say, tucking a curl behind her ear. I like being here to take care of her. I wouldn't have wanted her to be alone.

She emerges from the shower thirty minutes later while I'm setting up my bed on the couch. I freeze. Her damp curls frame her face, and she's only wearing one of Cal's oversized t-shirts that hits just below the curve of her ass. I have to grip the couch cushion to keep from reaching for her. Fuck. I need to stop looking at her like that—she just spent the day recovering from a hangover, and I'm thinking about what's under her t-shirt.

"Why didn't I do that sooner? I feel like a new woman," she says, shaking her fingers through her wet curls. A move that causes her shirt to hike dangerously high.

"Good." I focus on arranging my pillows, not the expanse of exposed flesh of her thighs.

"Okay then," she says at the doorway to Cal's room. "Thanks again for taking such good care of me. I owe you."

"It was my pleasure," I say.

She looks like she wants to say more, her eyes searching my face. For a heartbeat, neither of us moves, and the air between us feels electric. Then she goes into the bedroom and shuts the door behind her.

I stretch out on the couch and lace my fingers behind my head, staring at the ceiling. I hear the bedroom door click again.

"Liam," she says, reappearing from the bedroom. "You look ridiculous on that couch. You don't even fit." She glances back into Cal's room. "Cal's bed is huge. I'm sure we can share. We'll make a pillow wall." She turns to walk back into the room.

I freeze. Does she want me to follow? Was that an invitation?

"Liam," she pokes her head back out, "come to bed."

Chapter 10

Sophie

I wake with his arm draped over the curve of my hip, our pillow wall shoved to the floor at some point in the night. I'm the little spoon pressed into his sturdy chest, my ass squarely in his lap. But his breathing is long and steady with sleep, so I don't move.

Not that I want to.

Despite waking up with the worst hangover I've ever had, yesterday was one of my favorite days I can remember in a long time. Talking with Liam was so easy, I didn't feel like I had to put on an act around him. Plus, he'd now seen me throw up and didn't run the other way; he just held my hair and handed me a cold washcloth. I think that makes us official friends. Like he's no longer Cal's best friend, he's now mine too.

Except I was having more-than-friendly feelings towards him.

And maybe he was too?

I had thought he was about to kiss me when we got back from Bar None the other night. But we had both had too much to drink, and I didn't want to do anything either of us would regret.

But now we're both sober, and his hand is making slow, deliberate circles on the bare skin of my thigh. I don't want him to stop, not even a little.

All day, the line between friends and more seemed to blur. During our *Survivor* marathon, I hadn't meant to end up pressed against him like that, but each episode found me drifting closer until I was tucked into his side like I belonged there. When he reached out to tuck that curl behind my ear, his fingers lingered longer than necessary. I may or may not have intentionally left my sleep shorts on the bathroom floor after my shower, just to gauge his reaction. And the way he gripped that couch cushion, like he was having to physically restrain himself from taking me right there in the living room.

And I would have let him.

I feel him stir behind me, and I pretend to be asleep.

"Shit," he mutters as he removes his hand from my body. I miss its weight. The bed shifts as Liam rolls to his back, trying to put a little distance between us. I open one eye to peek at the expanse of bed in front of me, meaning I'm clearly over the line on 'his' side of the bed. He has to be falling off the edge.

I roll over so I'm facing him. "Hey," I say, my voice hoarse with sleep.

Liam tries to shift away. "I'm sorry. I didn't mean to—"

"No need to apologize. I think I am the bed hog here." I scoot back, reluctant to move too far away from the cozy heat radiating from his body. "I think I stole the bed that first night, too."

"Oh god, Soph, I am still so sorry about that night. I was drunk, and you were..." He rolls onto his side so he's facing me and swallows, his voice deeper, "you were kinda in my lap."

"I didn't mind," I say, my pulse ticking up. "I was surprised it was you, but...I liked it."

Liam shifts under the covers, like he doesn't want me to see that he needs to adjust himself.

I know Liam's reputation. While he doesn't post on social media, @therealliamblake is tagged with a different scantily clad woman every weekend. I know he doesn't do the relationship thing. But maybe that's better. I'm not looking for a relationship—after Marshall, who knows if I ever want a boyfriend again. But sex? I could go for that right now. Everything about Liam—his body, his hands, his cocky confidence, and the way he cares—makes me think he knows exactly what he's doing in bed. And maybe that is what I need right now.

I know he still thinks of me as Cal's little sister. But there's heat behind his eyes, and his body clearly responds to mine. He might just need permission to view me as...more.

"Do you remember what you said?" I push down the nervous lump in my throat. "That first night?" Because I sure as hell do, *let me touch you, baby. Let me make you come.*

Liam sucks in a breath, but doesn't move, and doesn't break our stare.

Finally, he tips his head once in acknowledgement. "I remember what I said."

"Do you think you can?"

"What are you asking me, Soph?" Liam asks, his voice low and gravelly.

"If you meant it."

I can see the debate behind his eyes as he struggles to find the right words. "You're Cal's little sister," he says finally, voice rough.

"I am, but I'm not a little girl anymore. I'm more than Cal's sister." I trace my finger across the ridge of his collarbone.

"You are not making this easier," he huffs out at my touch.

"But I am, Liam. I'm telling you this isn't on you to decide. I can make my own decisions. I don't need his permission. Neither do you."

Liam reaches out and runs his thumb over my bottom lip, and I want to pull it into my mouth.

"Ask me again," he almost growls.

"Do you think you can make me come?"

"Are you challenging me?" There is a tiny, delighted hitch in his voice, and he leans a little closer, twirling a curl around his finger and giving a tug.

"Most guys can't," I say, my voice emboldened, but my insides are fluttering with nerves. "I usually fake it, then take care of myself later."

"Most guys can't?" he asks. Our lips are so close they are almost touching. "Or the idiots you've been with don't take the time to figure out how you work?"

"And you would?"

Liam shifts, letting go of my hair and pushing up to his knees. "Show me."

"What?" I stammer, but the heat pooling between my legs tells me my body knows exactly what he just asked.

Liam tugs the comforter off me, his gaze flicking over the bare skin of my thighs. His bottom lip catches between his teeth, the pink going pale under the pressure. He swallows hard and sits back on his heels.

"Show me how to make you come."

Chapter 11

Liam

Sophie gasps softly, and I worry I might have gone too far. But the skin across her chest flushes a faint pink, and her breath quickens. I ring her ankle with my hand, keeping my gaze locked with hers the whole time.

"You are one hundred percent in control here, Soph. You can stop at any time," I say, moving her leg into a wider V. Her oversized shirt is still hiding most of her body, but when I widened her legs, her pale pink underwear appears where the hem lifted. "I've been thinking about making you come since I woke up with your ass in my lap that first night. But I want you to teach me how you like it." I release her ankle and reposition myself between her legs. "I promise I'm an excellent student."

I don't move. I don't touch her. Hell, I barely breathe. I can almost see the gears in her head turning before she pulls her bottom lip between her teeth and fingers the hem of her t-shirt.

"That's right, sweetheart. Show me what you do when you're alone. When that douchebag would leave you unsatisfied."

She closes her eyes and sits back against the headboard. My already hard dick is almost painful now, demanding to be let out. But I take a long inhale as she spreads her creamy thighs for me.

Her hand drags up her body over her breasts, nipples peaking beneath the thin fabric of her t-shirt. She moves a hand under her shirt, and although the fabric hides her, I can tell when she traces a thumb across her nipple, pinching then arching her back and letting out a little moan that I feel in my core.

"God, you like that, don't you?" I breathe out.

Her hand trails over the soft swell of her belly, gripping the hem of her shirt and pulling it over her head. Both breasts bounce free, and I almost lose it just at the sight of her absolutely perfect, round tits. She takes her time, clearly enjoying her breasts as much as I am watching. She squeezes full handfuls and tugs on her nipples, kneading and increasing the pressure. When she lets out a breathy gasp, I almost wonder if she's already made herself come, but soon her fingers trace across the top seam of her underwear, one finger dipping inside.

My gaze flicks to her face, but she is somewhere else. Her eyes are still closed, her lower lip caught between her teeth, and she's either forgotten I'm here or she's putting on one hell of a show. But as she lifts her hips and wriggles out of her underwear, her eyes open, her gaze locked on me, before she tosses them into my lap. A wicked grin spreads across her face, and she spreads her legs wide, exposing herself completely to me.

Okay, then. Putting on a show.

"That's right, baby, show me," I growl.

She wastes no time now and drags two fingers up and down through her folds until they glisten.

"Fuck," I mutter. And her lip tips in a sly smile before she slides her fingers back down her center, dipping them both inside and pausing with a ragged inhale.

I'm mesmerized by her fingers dipping in and out, while her thumb applies a steady pressure to her clit. Her heels dig into the bed, and her hips tip up slightly, trying to seek more pressure from her hand. She plunges her fingers in deep now, and I use her underwear to palm myself through my shorts. Her breath becomes labored, and I can tell she's close. It's all I can do not to take over and dive between her legs, but I just watch—riveted.

"Oh," she lets out another breathy gasp as she picks up her speed, a determined grimace on her face, and I nearly come in my shorts.

"Yeah, baby," I rasp out. "Show me how you come."

She rubs her clit in fast, tight circles, arching off the bed as she cries out.

She collapses back onto the bed, stretching her legs out and twisting her body as she comes down from her high. Her breathing slows, and a lazy smile spreads across her face.

"I think I understand," I say, my voice hoarse. Her eyes open as I crawl towards her still-open legs.

"Now?" she gasps.

"Only if you want, baby."

"I can't. I mean, I've never."

"Never what?"

"Twice, even by myself."

"But I had such an excellent teacher," I muse, lowering myself to my belly between her knees.

"Liam," she warns, but she doesn't close her legs. I kiss the inside of her thigh.

"Like I said, you are in control. We can stop any time, but I would very much like to make you come." I kiss higher up her inner thigh. "Again."

"Okay, but—" I can feel her body tense. I stop and pull back, giving her space.

"Hey, look at me, sweetheart." She gazes down at me with her doe eyes, still a little post-orgasm drunk. "We can stop. That was already the best show I've ever seen in my life."

"No!" She reaches, catching me by the shirt, and I can't help but laugh. "I just don't know if I can," she says, fingering the fabric, "you know, finish...again."

"How about you just enjoy yourself, and we'll see where we end up?"

She nods and then actually smiles, draping her arm over her eyes.

"What?"

"I've just never been this open in talking about sex, you know."

"I think communication is pretty sexy," I tell her. And while I never fuck around when it comes to consent, I've never wanted to actually learn how to please someone more than I do right now. And not for some bullshit toxic masculinity reason like I'm the only guy who can make her come, but because she deserves it. She deserves a guy who will take the time to figure out how to make her happy—

I mean, how to make her come. I can do that. I can make her come.

"Okay," Sophie says, breaking into my thoughts that were veering severely off course. "I think your head was down here somewhere." She closes her eyes and gestures between her legs.

"Yes, ma'am," I say. I settle between her legs and twirl my fingers through her folds.

"Oh my god," she whimpers when I dip two fingers inside, just like she had, although I pause to let her body soften to my larger digits. When her body relaxes around me, I replicate the exact rhythm she used. Her breathy little moans tell me how to adjust my pressure and pace accordingly.

"Yes, Liam," she gasps when I've found her perfect rhythm.

I kiss the inside of her thigh again, while I pump my fingers in and out of her until they are so slippery they make a debaucherous squelching sound that makes my cock somehow even harder. Instead of my thumb, I press my tongue flat against her clit. She lets out that same throaty moan I've been dying to hear again since I woke up that first night with her in my arms. I suck her into my mouth and flick my tongue. When she shifts her thighs, I follow her subtle guidance on my location, never slowing the rhythm of my fingers inside of her.

"Oh, God, yes," she cries out, and I lock in on exactly what I'm doing. Like, I don't change a single thing.

Her entire body convulses, and she unravels on my tongue while I watch from between the V of her legs.

Chapter 12

Sophie

"So I've been thinking about Andy's parents," I say, launching into the speech I'd been rehearsing since about five minutes after my first-ever two-in-a-row orgasmic experience at four am.

I've caught Liam glancing at me more than once over his laptop this morning, trying to be casual, but there's something different in the air between us—charged but careful, like we're both trying to figure out what last night means.

"Yeah?" he says from his usual spot on the couch, drinking the latte I made him when I woke up. It's become our morning routine—I make us lattes because Liam can't seem to wrap his head around a multi-step coffee process.

"I just usually pour mine out of a pot," he told me one of the first mornings, when I found him jabbing buttons on the gleaming chrome machine like it had mortally offended him.

As was also our morning routine, Liam had been awake long before I woke up in Cal's bed. Alone.

He's in his running gear, his shirt clinging to his chest in a way that makes it hard to look away. But my eyes catch on the rumple of blankets next to him. Had he retreated to the couch? I won't lie, I hoped I'd wake up with him still there, his body wrapped around mine–or with his head between my legs.

Last night was fantastic. Earth-shattering, to put it mildly. I've had sex before, plenty, honestly. Everyone in art school seemed to double major in oil paints and casual hookups. But this felt different.

Liam hadn't been kidding when he said he was a good student. He didn't just *watch* me—he studied me. Learned my body like my pleasure was the whole point, not just a stop on the way to the main event. Within minutes, he figured out things most guys never even tried to notice.

I want that again. I crave more sensations and want to discover new experiences in bed that I am pretty sure only he could provide. I also want to learn all the nuances of his body. He hadn't taken off his clothes. He didn't come. We didn't even kiss on the mouth.

It seems a shame for it to be only a one-night thing.

I shut my laptop and gather my courage. "That Andy's parents believe that sex and love are two different things."

Liam chokes on a sip of coffee. "I thought you were going to say how wild it was that Andy never went to traditional school and that her mom's a contortionist," Liam replies, wiping the dribble of coffee off his chin.

"I just think Andy made a good point that sex doesn't have to come with all the relationship baggage," I hop down from the stool. "If both parties agree."

Liam's eyes flash with hesitation, but also something that looks a lot like desire. "I'm not sure I'm following..." he says, but his voice is low.

"We're going to be stuck in this apartment together for the next few weeks. We're both single, and frankly, I'd rather stick a needle under my fingernail than get on the dating apps." I try to keep my voice light, but I have to turn away from the steady intensity of Liam's gaze, now locked on me, to finish my speech. "We get along, we're adults, we're clearly attracted to each other...let's just...agree to have sex."

Liam lets out a low grunt behind me—probably meant to sound indignant, but it comes out way too heated for me to backpedal on my proposal.

"Neither of us wants a relationship. This can be another perk of our accidental cohabitation. Like custom-made lattes and salmon bowls. We add on-demand orgasms."

"Sophie," he breathes out my name on a laugh, his eyes still locked on me, a curious smile tugging at his lips. We fall quiet, both waiting to see who moves first. My heart pounds behind my ribs, and I silently beg him not to notice how nervous I am beneath all my bravado. Nervous, he might actually say no.

"Okay..." he says, dragging his hand over his mouth. "How would this work?"

Something electric zips under my skin.

"It's just sex. No one gets attached." I explain. "But we agree not to sleep with anyone else. I don't do non-monogamy, even casually. And if one of us meets someone else—"

"We stop."

"Exactly," I agree. "And we don't tell Cal."

A breath leaves Liam in a heavy rush as he crosses to the window and pushes it open. "Soph," he says, staring down at the street, "I don't think this is a good idea."

"The friends with benefits agreement, or not telling my brother?"

"I can't keep something like that from Cal. He doesn't even know you are here, much less that we are both here...together. But at this point, I can still face him without deserving a black eye."

"So you are going to tell him about last night?"

He grips the back of his neck, but doesn't answer.

"Oh, Cal, BTW," I mock. "I gave your little sister the best orgasm of her life...in your bed."

"Fuck, you're right." He pinches his temple, but then adds quietly, "The best?" He's still looking out the window, but I catch the little smirk he's trying to hide.

I wait for him to look back at me before confirming with a tip of my chin. And the look on Liam's face—half sheepish grin and half cocky pride—does something low in my belly. "Just sex, no strings, no one else." I hold out my hand for him to shake. "And we don't tell Cal."

Chapter 13

Liam

When I get back from my run, Sophie's gone.

And so is the heap of art supplies by the door.

The past three days have been a masterclass in sexual tension. We've been circling each other, both waiting for the other to make a move. Yesterday, we both froze after her hip brushed my thigh in the kitchen. The day before, I walked out of the shower in just a towel and caught her staring at my chest like she wanted to taste the water running down. But neither of us goes further. We made this deal, but neither of us seems to know how to start it—and now I'm afraid she's gotten sick of the awkwardness and left.

I panic and dart into Cal's room, but her duffel bag remains on the chair in the corner, her shoes are sitting at the foot of the bed, and her toiletries are a jumble on the dresser. I exhale. Thank fuck, she didn't leave.

This morning, when she caught me staring at her legs while she did yoga in the living room, her sly little smile made my dick hard, but did she want to have sex right then? Part of me wanted to throw her over my shoulder and carry her into Cal's room to finish what we'd started three nights ago. But I opted to burn off some steam the old-fashioned way, by pounding out five miles through Golden Gate Park.

But I thought of Sophie the entire run.

I thought about her sharp tongue and those dangerous curves I want to get lost in, and the best breathy moans when I make her come.

Something I've apparently now agreed to do "on demand," and I'm not even a little bit mad about it. As much as I hate keeping secrets from Cal—he's the only one I told before Sophie about getting cut from the Iron Cats—Sophie's right. This is just for a few weeks, a casual convenience, and Cal doesn't need to know all my business, especially if it will be over before he even gets home. Sophie was clear she didn't want anything more, and eventually, I'll have to find a real job and a place to live. This is like the summer after your senior year of college—a last chance to enjoy yourself before entering the real world. Apparently, only my version involves sleeping with my incredibly hot roommate.

Who is now gone.

While I'm relatively certain she didn't change her mind and move out, I still wonder where she is. Not that she has to tell me where she's going. That wasn't part of the agreement, right? *Dude, get it together. She does not owe you anything.*

I take a shower, and when I get out, there's a message on my phone.

Sophie: *not sure if you're back, but I'm on the roof*

I didn't even know this building had roof access, but suddenly I'm heading for the door. I pull it open with more force than necessary.

"Oh!" the woman across the hall gasps. "What the fuck?"

"Sorry," I apologize sheepishly to Harper, Cal's workaholic neighbor. The one who caught Sophie and me almost kissing that night. "I was rushing to meet someone."

"Do you plan on bringing another random woman back to your friend's apartment?" Harper asks, clutching a glass food container as she heads toward the stairs.

"She wasn't random," I say, following her up. I stop short of adding that it was Cal's sister—who knows what he's told her, or what she'd report back. "If you'll excuse me." I nod and slip past her up the stairs.

I step onto the rooftop deck, expecting to find Sophie curled up on the lounger with the smutty paperback I always see her reading, eating straight from a bag of Cool Ranch Doritos, sipping a Diet Coke. What I don't expect is what I find her doing instead.

She's painting.

She has her easel set up near the wall facing the city skyline, wild curls catching in the afternoon breeze. Her paints spill out of her antique-looking tackle box, tubes and little jars scattered everywhere. I can see her in profile, paint flecked across her full cheeks and the bridge of her pert nose. Her brush races across the canvas. She doesn't see me. Doesn't hear me. She's completely lost to the world. For a second, I don't breathe.

She's stunning like this. Not just her—though, hell, yes, her—but the confidence in her movements. The way the colors burst across her canvas with such wild, unrestrained passion. Her hands move so quickly, I can't believe there's any method to her madness, but I can also clearly see how the San Francisco skyline transforms from reality in front of her onto her canvas. Not a realistic recreation, but an almost otherworldly interpretation of...the feeling of the skyline. All done in shades of blue and teal, along with other colors I don't have the vocabulary to describe.

This isn't just talent. It's fucking magic.

She's wearing an oversized men's dress shirt as a well-used paint smock, and the metallic taste of jealousy coats my tongue at the thought of whoever wore it before her. Of whomever she stole it from, maybe after it was discarded on a bedroom floor.

Something shifts deep in my chest.

When she finally glances over, surprised, I lift a hand, a little sheepish.

"Don't stop," I say softly. "I like watching you work."

She watches me for a few long beats, and I think I've ruined the moment—that I've broken whatever spell she was under. But soon, she turns back to the canvas, her brush beginning to move again. Slower, but no less deliberate.

I settle into the lounge chairs and just...watch.

I lose track of time, caught in the rhythm of her process. She finally steps back from the canvas and cocks her head, taking in her creation.

"I haven't painted in eighteen months," she says, and I'm not sure if it's a statement or an apology.

"Why now?"

Her lips curve, thoughtful. "I'm not sure." She drifts closer, closing the space between us. Her oversized shirt swallows whatever she's wearing beneath it, leaving only the sleek lines of her thighs on display. Before I can process it, she's climbing onto the lounger, straddling me. My hands find her hips like they are magnets.

"I think I remembered what it feels like to want something just because I want it, not because I'm supposed to."

She reaches a paint-stained hand out to cup my cheek. Our eyes lock. A beat passes. Then she's kissing me—slow, deliberate, just like her brushstrokes. My fingers dig into her waist, pulling her down onto my lap. She lets out a little sigh when she makes contact with my erection, which I think has been there since I stepped onto this roof forty-five minutes ago or maybe since I woke with her in my arms that first night.

She smells a little like paint but mostly like lemon cookies, and I want to suck on her neck to see if she tastes that way too. However, I can't stop kissing her. We didn't kiss that night in Cal's bed, and now I regret not knowing for the past three days how perfect her mouth is.

She finally breaks the kiss. Seeing how swollen and flushed her lips are makes a spot behind my ribs ache. But I reach out and thumb the open collar of her shirt instead.

"Is this Mr. Artsy McDouchebag's shirt?" I smirk, but I want to punch her ex in the face.

"No," she chuckles, "it's my dad's. I've used it for years."

I nudge her back with a grin. "Way to kill the mood—kind of hard to make out with you in the shirt of the guy who taught me how to shave."

"We can take care of that," she says, undoing the button and revealing she's not wearing much under that shirt. A lacy bra that barely contains her breasts and the tiniest pair of denim cut-offs that can still count as shorts.

"Fuck," I mutter as she lets the shirt drop off her shoulders, and I pull her back to me. I plunge my tongue into her mouth and palm her breasts, unable to keep my hands off them. Her hands roam the contours of my chest and down my abs until she finds the button of my jeans. "Should we go downstairs?" I murmur against her mouth.

She shakes her head. "No. Here is fine." And my insides drop.

She drags her mouth away from mine and pops the button on my jeans. My erection strains against the fabric of my briefs, and her smile turns devilish as she hooks the elastic with her paint-flecked fingers. My cock springs free like a fucking jack-in-the-box, and an ego-boosting "oh" escapes her lips.

She wraps her delicate fingers around my length, giving me a few firm tugs before shimmying down my body, and my entire life flashes before my eyes.

She looks up at me through her thick lashes and locks eyes with mine before her tongue darts out to lick the drop of pre-cum leaking out of the tip.

"Fuck," I moan, but I can't tear my eyes away from Sophie's mouth. I watch in complete awe as she swirls her tongue over the head like a fucking ice cream cone. Then she licks down the side and drags her tongue flat from the base to the tip. Swirling at the top again before adding her hand, wrapping tightly around my base, and squeezing with the exact perfect amount of pressure.

I swear again as I thread my hand into her hair and fist my grip at the base of her skull. This time, the moan escapes *her* lips, and she sinks onto me, taking me into her wet, hot mouth.

"Soph," I grit, arching into her mouth, my grip tightening in her hair, but she is in control. Of the pace, of the pressure, of every sensation as she glides up and down over my shaft. I'm not going to last. "Honey," I warn, as my stomach muscles clench. But she just moans, her lips vibrating against the sensitive underside. I try to guide her gently back by the hair, but she picks up her pace, bobbing her head with the most delightful slurping sound. "I'm going to..."

"Yes, do it," she commands before taking me impossibly deep, and I explode against the back of her throat. My body convulses, my hips buck involuntarily, and she takes it all, swallowing me down. Not breaking her pace, her hands massage and squeeze while her perfect mouth takes every last drop.

She looks up at me, her eyes glistening with tears and a wicked smile. I glance over her shoulder at her painting, the fading sun, the golden light catching in her hair. She wipes the corner of her mouth in a way that is somehow both crude and incredibly sexy before climbing up my body to kiss me, deep and intentional.

Something in my chest shifts, and I realize I'm in deep shit.

This was supposed to be simple.

Chapter 14

Sophie

We tumble back into the apartment, all laughter and hands everywhere. I would have stayed on the roof, but Liam couldn't stand the idea of anyone else seeing me naked when I tried to shimmy out of my shorts on his lap.

"Besides, I'm thirty-one, Soph," he'd said, still breathless after coming down from his orgasm. "Give an old man a refractory period."

I'd thrown my paints back into the art box, and when I looked up, Liam was just staring at my painting.

"I can't believe you turned all those scattered tubes into *this*," he said, staring at the messy, abstract skyline I'd painted almost involuntarily. It had felt like a trance—like the art was channeling through me, not something I was consciously *producing*.

Finally.

Now, back in the apartment, Liam comes up behind me, wraps his arms around my waist, and trails his mouth down the column of my throat.

My whole life has felt calculated—every move part of someone else's long-term vision. Professors, art critics, Marshall—they all had ideas of what I should become. I needed something I was completely in control of.

I need to get out of my head and just feel. This thing with Liam—it's the perfect distraction. No stakes, no strings.

"Your body is unreal," he murmurs into my neck, hands wandering under my hastily buttoned shirt before spinning me in his arms to face him.

"Are you ready, old man?" I laugh.

He huffs. "I was ready the moment I got your perfect tits in my hands."

"Hey, I know we talked about not sleeping with anyone else, but I've been tested and I'm clear," I say, and Liam pulls back from kissing my neck to look at me.

"The team doctors test us every month," he explains, tucking a curl behind my ear. "But I haven't slept with anyone in months, anyway."

"I still want to use condoms," I tell him.

"Of course," he says. "My mom had me at fifteen. Safe sex has been drilled into me since I could talk."

"Okay, then," I say.

"Hey," he wraps a hand around the nape of my neck, but uses his thumb on my jaw to still me. "We don't have to do this. Consent is a continuous conversation. You can change your mind."

"Oh, I want to." That isn't the problem. It's that I can't believe how much I want to, and I worry that might be the problem.

I close the distance between us and press my lips to his. He tastes like mint, and I can still smell the citrusy body wash from his shower. I tug at the hem of his shirt, and he lets me pull it off. I take in the slope of his broad chest, the long line of his shoulder, and each ridge of his abs—a body honed since childhood to perform at an elite level. I kiss the hard slope of his chest muscle and let my tongue drag across his nipple.

"Fuck," he lets out, reaching under my shirt to squeeze my breasts. "I need you naked."

He walks me backwards to the bedroom, undoing the two shirt buttons I managed to close, pushing it off my shoulders. My breath catches, and my breasts feel heavy with want. He gazes down at me like he can't believe I'm real.

"Wait here," he says, like there is anywhere else I'd want to be right now.

He returns with a strip of condoms in a gold foil package, and suddenly the thought of him, of his cock, inside me both thrills and terrifies me. I could barely get my lips around him on the rooftop. Marshall had been nowhere near his size, and even my most impressive vibrator couldn't prepare me for what was under Liam's briefs.

He catches the look on my face, and a soft smile spreads across his lips. He tosses the condoms onto the bed. "We'll take our time," he assures. "Can I get you naked?"

I nod and unclasp my bra.

"Fuck, Soph." Liam moans, almost whines, as my bra drops to the floor. His gaze travels across my body before he bends and pulls a taut nipple into his mouth, twirling his tongue around the stiff bud. He mumbles something that sounds like "uh-huh" before biting down just this side of painful.

"Oh!" I gasp, but arch my hips into him, looking for friction. He licks the spot he just bit, soothing with his tongue. His fingers trail down my body to the button of my shorts, and he slides his hands around to knead the curve of my ass, letting my shorts pool on the ground. I begin to grind when he pulls me against his thigh, and the denim of his jeans rough and perfect against the thin cotton of my panties.

There are sensations everywhere. My skin sparks everywhere he touches me, and yet it's still not enough.

"Please," I beg, undoing the button of his jeans and shoving them off his hips. His erection strains against the fabric of his black boxers. I reach for him, but he stills my hand.

"Not yet, I want you to come in my mouth." He pulls my face to his, kissing me thoroughly before nipping at my lower lip. "I need to taste you."

He tugs me towards the bed, but lies back against the mattress first. He hooks a hand around my knee, and I realize the position he wants me in.

"Liam, I'll smother you." I laugh.

"I can bench press two-eighty as a warm-up, sweetheart, don't insult me." He says with a wicked laugh. "Now get over here and sit on my face."

I can feel the color spread across my cheeks at his words, but I also know I'm already soaked, and he's barely touched me.

He does this to me. He makes me feel brave and safe and daring, all with just a sly look or a subtle tip of his chin. He makes me want to try, and he makes me want to trust him—and maybe trust myself for the first time in a long time.

I shimmy out of my underwear before kneeling on the bed and swinging my knee over, mounting Liam like a motorcycle.

"That's perfect, sweetheart," he says from beneath the spread of my legs, his eyes flicking to the headboard. "Now, hold on."

I do as I'm told, desperate to have his mouth on me again. I lean forward to grip the headboard and settle my ass back, and I'm rewarded with his hot mouth on my slick center. His tongue moves unhurriedly from my entrance to my clit and back down again. I am so close, just from a few passes, that I have to grip the headboard, knuckles white, and breathe to keep from instantly orgasming.

He licks long and slow and exquisite. And when he slides in a finger, then two, my hips rock against his hand like someone else is pulling the strings, and yet somehow, I'm wildly in control of every sensation.

His long fingers arch inside, and his mouth sucks and flicks me in a way that is so perfect, it's like he's done it a million times. He knows exactly how to strum me.

I'm so wet that when he slips a third finger in, I hardly notice until I feel the delightful stretch. "Oh, fuck, yes."

He huffs out a grunt, vibrating against my heat-slicked core, before thrusting deeper. He curls his fingers, twisting his wrist like he's unlocking a key, and in so many ways, he is.

He's teasing and worshiping and stretching me. When I realize he's preparing my body to take him, I lose it.

"Liam!" I cry out as my orgasm crashes around me. His grip on my hip tightens, and he holds me to his mouth, drawing my orgasm out until my legs begin to shake.

I climb off of him, trying to catch my breath, and he pulls my mouth to his. I can taste myself on his lips, and I want more. My hand dips below the waistband of his boxers to pull out his length.

"I'm ready," I say, giving him a long, firm stroke. "I want you inside me."

I take the foil package and roll the condom on. His cock is almost obscene.

"You're in control, sweetheart," he says, guiding me back onto his lap. "Take as much or as little as you want. It's already perfect."

Nothing about him is little.

I slot his head at my entrance, and my body is thrumming with desire, and my heart is pounding so fast I'm sure he can hear it.

"That's it, honey, nice and slow," he praises as I sink inch by inch over his cock. The sweet sting of the stretch causes heat to bloom in my stomach. I know this will be devastating, and I want every second of it.

His hands cup under my ass. He's letting me control the pace and depth, but he's bearing all my weight.

"Touch yourself," he says, and my hand finds my clit like a reflex.

It's disorienting in the best way—how he takes charge while still making me feel completely in control. He knows what he wants, but my pleasure is paramount. I press quick, deliberate circles on the bundle of nerves, and as wet as I thought I was, I'm able to sink a little lower, take more of him, with this new stimulation.

"That's it, sweetheart, look how well you're taking me."

His praise does something molten to my insides, and I pick up my pace. We begin to climb together, and he alternates between little swears and admiration. Sweat glistens on my forehead, and my thighs burn, even though Liam is doing most of the work. He rocks into me. And everything about this is ruinous. His body moving in mine, the stretch of him, the dig of his fingers into the flesh of my hip. It's pure pleasure, the kind you crave again the moment it ends. And I don't want it to.

"Come for me, sweetheart."

And I do. Over and over. I cry out, and every nerve ending is sparking like a downed live wire. There is no way this can be classified as a single orgasm. Tears prick the corners of my eyes, not from pain or discomfort, but from pleasure and deep, satisfying contentment. Like Liam somehow shattered me and made me whole at the same time. My pleasure crashes over me again in waves, and soon, Liam is swearing and bucking his hips underneath me, before shuddering inside me.

"Fuck, Soph...Fuck..." he grits out, his fingers dig into my hips, gripping me to him as his desperation rolls through every ragged exhale.

I collapse against his chest, and he gathers me in his arms, our bodies sticky with sweat.

And this is exactly how I want to be undone.

Chapter 15
Liam

I've just hit a homerun, and the buzz of the crowd is so wild my ears are ringing. I'm playing ball again, but this isn't the baseball dream I've had a million times since I was ten. This one is about Sophie. She is there in the stands. And when the game is over, we have celebratory sex in the back of my car in the players' parking lot. And as hot as hell that part of the dream is, the best part is when we finish, we drive home together. To our house.

Something buzzes again, and I realize it's not the crowd, and I'm not dreaming. I reach across the expanse of sheets to find her. To haul her into me. To get my mouth on her again.

The phone rings again, and I crack one eye open at the nightstand.

Cal Rhodes is FaceTiming you.

Fuck.

I bolt upright and grab my phone, clutching it to my chest like Cal could see who I'm with through the unanswered phone. But as I frantically look to my right, I realize I'm alone.

The phone rings again.

Fuck.

Then I hear the shower running in the hall. It strikes me that Sophie is up earlier than usual. But Cal's nagging ringtone pulls my attention. If I answer and Sophie walks in wearing just her towel…or less…we're both dead. But if I don't answer, Cal will think something's wrong. I know he was worried about me when he left. And I was pretty fucked up, so I don't blame him. If I don't answer now, he'll do something drastic like call my mom.

Fuck.

I need to answer, assure him everything is cool here, and get off the phone before Sophie gets out of the shower. I hit accept.

"Dude!" Cal's voice booms out of my phone, making me recoil back from the screen.

"Hey, man, what's up? How's Cancun?" I say, trying to sound as nonchalant as possible.

"Cambodia, dude. You're still in bed? What time is it there? I thought it was like 8 a.m.?"

"Um, yeah," I run my fingers through my hair. "It is."

"What happened to your crack of dawn runs?"

"I just…" I stammer into the phone, my eyes flicking to the bedroom door.

"Oh, fuck me. You have a girl there, don't you? Or more than one?"

"No!" I say a little too forcefully. "What?"

"Dude, you are still in bed at eight and you have the 'I had a girl riding my face all night' hair."

"Fuck off." But there's a little too much heat in my voice, so I try to add a laugh at the end.

"What? It's cool, man. I'm glad my bed is seeing some action. You've probably had more girls in there since I left than I've ever had."

My eyes flick to the door again. *Please, Sophie, don't come out of the bathroom.*

"Oh, wait, is she still there? That's unlike you. You usually have them out the door before they can catch their breath."

My mind wanders to last night. The way Sophie's body felt curled around mine, soft and luscious. Her little mewls of pleasure. The way she smelled, a little like a sugar cookie and a lot like me. And I loved how she fucking tasted. And the way I felt inside her, like my body was made to fit. Despite Cal's accurate description of my habits, when we were done, I didn't want to go anywhere. I pulled her on top of me and stroked her hair until we both fell asleep. I wonder when she'd gotten up? I had hoped we could spend the whole day in this bed, enjoying this thing—this agreement—between us.

"Earth to Liam, sorry to break into your sex dream there, but..."

"Did you call all the way from...wherever the fuck you are to harass me about who I'm sleeping with?"

"No, no, you're right. But did you at least get this one's name?"

"I'm hanging up on you. I don't care if this is your one phone call for the month."

"I'm staffing a rural health clinic, not a prison."

I shrug into the phone. "Sounds like the same thing."

Cal laughs with the familiar boom to his voice.

"Well, you look good," Cal says, nodding in approval. "Whether it's copious amounts of anonymous sex or not, you look more like yourself. I was really worried about you when I left."

Cal has been my ride or die since I was fourteen, and as much shit as we give each other, he's never let me down. And here I am lying to his face. I should tell him. I should come clean. But I promised Sophie I wouldn't say anything to her brother. I can't break her trust like that either. It's loud wherever Cal is calling from, and I strain to hear if the shower is still running over the din. I don't want Sophie to walk in right now.

"Thanks, man," I say, but my eyes dart around the room.

I try to angle the phone away from the door, but Sophie's stuff is everywhere. If I move at all, Cal will see her clothes, her art supplies, and her teddy bear that she's had since she was a kid, Mr. Snowflake, on the dresser. If Cal sees any of it, he'll know.

"Liam, what's going on there?" Cal's voice changes. It shifts from the teasing tone he's been using to one that is filled with that classic Cal Rhodes big brother concern. "Are you okay? Wait. Who's there with you?"

He knows. He fucking knows. He knows his little sister is here, and he knows I've been taking advantage of her. I don't know how, but he knows.

"Nothing," I let out a long sigh, like I'm getting bored with this conversation. "You're right, I had someone here last night, but it's no big deal." I stare at Cal through the phone. My heart is beating so wildly, I'm sure he can see it through my bare chest, but I keep my expression neutral. "You know me. It's just sex, it doesn't mean anything."

Chapter 16
Sophie

I stand naked in the turned-off shower, unable to move or even breathe.

I could hear my brother's booming voice even over the drone of the water, but I had to hear what he was saying and, more importantly, what Liam was admitting to.

"You have a girl there, don't you?" I can hear my brother say through the wall.

How could I forget Liam was incapable of keeping a secret from my brother? Back in tenth grade, he broke Cal's Lego Eiffel Tower. Cal assumed the cat did it and wasn't even mad, but Liam confessed everything within five minutes.

Of course he was going to tell Cal I was here, and probably—against his own self-interest—about our agreement.

Our agreement.

Our agreement was supposed to be casual. No emotions. No stakes. But last night didn't feel that way. The way he figured out exactly what I craved and gave it to me, again and again. The way he touched me—like I wasn't fragile, but he could be the one to hold me together if I broke. And the way he clutched me to his chest afterward as if he was afraid I'd leave. Nothing about last night felt casual.

That wasn't what we agreed to.

When I woke up, our naked bodies still tangled together, I already knew I had to put some distance between us. That's why I got up to take a shower, and thank god I did. Thank god I was out of there before Cal called.

I carefully slide open the shower door and wrap myself in a towel. I lean against the closed door, straining to listen.

"You're right, I had someone here last night, but it's no big deal." Liam's voice is detached, and my stomach drops. This is where he tells him. "You know me. It's just sex, it doesn't mean anything."

Something in my chest cracks.

But I also exhale the breath I'd been holding since I heard the phone ring.

Liam didn't spill our secrets. But he did tell the truth. *It's just sex, it doesn't mean anything.*

This is why I suggested the agreement. Liam Blake doesn't do relationships. He's the Playboy athlete who never gets attached—and that's why this works. Whatever I thought I felt last night is just sex. Really good sex I want to keep having. I just need to keep my boundaries in check. That's what we both want.

I pull on yesterday's leggings and the hoodie I left in the bathroom. I'm not walking back into Cal's room naked for clean clothes. I wait at the door until I'm sure Liam's off the phone with my brother, then head to the kitchen and grab the Froot Loops I've ignored ever since he started leaving egg sandwiches on the counter before his runs. He's not my boyfriend. If this FWB thing is going to work, I need some distance.

"Hey," Liam says, walking into the kitchen in just a pair of low-slung flannel pajama pants. He leans down to kiss my cheek, but I step back, reaching for the milk. Liam watches me, but he doesn't press. "How'd you sleep?"

"Great!" I say a little too chipper. "A good orgasm will do that to a girl." And not the curling up in the cocoon of his body heat all night.

"I...uh," Liam hesitates. "I talked to your brother while you were in the shower."

"Really?" I say. "How's he doing?"

Liam watches me pour milk into my cereal bowl and scratches at the stubble across his jaw. "He's good. They finished building the health clinic, and now he's seeing patients for the next eight weeks."

"Sounds like Cal," I say, digging through the drawer for my favorite spoon. Eight weeks. The past month has been fun pretending things are going smoothly, but Cal will be back in two months, this thing with Liam will be over, and I'll have to get on with my life—figure out what that even looks like now that my art career is off the table. I might be painting, but it's not the kind of art that sells, and I'm not sure I even want it to be anymore.

"I didn't tell him..." he says, pulling me out of my doom spiral. He shifts on his feet and studies the pile of Cal's mail on the breakfast bar like it might have some answers. "I didn't tell him you were here."

Relief washes over me. I need more time to sort everything out. I look up at Liam—the flush on his cheek, the bow of his lip, the hard line of his shoulder—and I'm hit with an uncontrollable urge to get lost in those muscled arms.

Maybe I can pretend for a bit longer.

"It's better this way," I reply, and take my Froot Loops into Cal's room, shutting the door behind me.

Chapter 17

Liam

Two weeks into this agreement, and I should be grateful she's keeping us on track.

At first, I was worried Sophie was having second thoughts. The way she slipped out before I woke up that first morning, how she disappeared into Cal's room after we talked about his call—I figured maybe she regretted the whole thing. I could have let it go, maybe not easily, but I could have gone back.

But a few nights later, while we were watching *Survivor*, she crawled between my knees and made me see stars. What I'd mistaken for second thoughts was clearly Sophie sticking to the rules we'd both agreed on. Just sex, no strings. I wasn't disappointed—this is exactly what I signed up for.

And the sex is incredible. The next time she was doing yoga in the living room—in her skimpiest shorts and strappiest bra—I rewarded her with an orgasm right there on her mat. One morning, when she was almost out the door for coffee with Liv and Andy, she asked if I had five minutes. I made her come so fast she wasn't even late.

But Sophie is determined to keep things purely physical. She started ignoring the egg sandwiches I made her until I quit leaving them. She blows my mind with her body, then is up and dressed before I can catch my breath. We don't linger, and we definitely don't have sex in Cal's bed again.

This should be exactly what I wanted—not to get caught up in all the relationship distractions. So why do I wish she'd let me hold her longer? It's fine. Cleaner this way. Whatever that first night was, it wasn't feelings. Just really good sex. I'm not sure I'd even know what *more* feels like.

"Shit," she mutters, clicking keys on her laptop one afternoon. I'd just gotten out of the shower and was going to suggest a quickie before I catch the concern in her eyes.

"What is it?" I ask.

"Oh, nothing." She glances over her shoulder at me, but doesn't seem to notice I'm only in my towel. "Just another reminder, I'm behind on my student loan payments."

"What about your content stuff?" I ask, pulling on my shorts. She's clearly not in the mood. "You seem to be working all the time."

"Yeah, but the pay is shit and inconsistent. I'm going to need to find something more stable soon."

"Yeah, you and me both."

She holds up her coffee mug. "Cheers to burned-out has-beens who can't make ends meet."

I huff out a laugh, but her assessment stings a little. I walk over to the kitchen and punch a few buttons on Cal's ridiculous coffee machine until I give up and grab a beer from the fridge. I turn around to see Sophie watching me, but she quickly looks down at her laptop.

"What about your painting?" I gesture across to the stack of canvases piling up against the living room wall. Skylines, landscapes, sunsets. Realistic, but all with a slightly different spin, different colors, perspectives, and sizes. She'd been painting every day, getting up early and lugging her supplies to the roof. I don't follow her anymore, and she doesn't invite me, but every day when she comes back down, paint-stained and sun-kissed, I swell with pride. I see the light in her eyes again, the one she was missing when she first showed up at Cal's.

"This isn't the kind of art that sells," she dismisses and turns back to her laptop.

I don't know anything about art, but I don't understand why not. I set my beer on the counter next to her and start folding a basket of my clean laundry.

"I was kind of thinking about maybe doing seasonal tax prep or something," I say, folding my t-shirts into a neat stack on the counter. I know what we agreed to, but I like this—working side by side, watching *Survivor* together, just hanging out even when we're not having sex. "I think there are certifications, but I haven't looked into it yet."

"But do you really want to spend all your time doing taxes?" She swivels her body on her stool to look at me.

"What else am I going to do?" I fold another t-shirt and notice her light pink sleep shorts and tank top have somehow found their way into my laundry. I don't mind. In fact, I like it more than I should. I fold the shorts into a tiny package and place them next to her.

"What about coaching?" She's watching me as I pull out a pair of lacy underwear and fold them once before adding them to her stack. "Or sports management? Or commentating?"

"Nah," I shake my head. "If I'm not playing, anything else just feels like...settling."

She's quiet long enough that I finally meet her gaze.

"Settling?" she asks.

"Like admitting I failed."

"You know that's not true, right? It's not failing, it's evolution. You love the game more than most people who are still playing."

"Maybe. But I've wasted enough time on a game that isn't loving me back. Taxes feel more...predictable."

"And boring as hell," she says, handing me the last t-shirt in my basket. "When was the last time you felt excited about a spreadsheet?"

"I don't know, Soph." I put the stack of folded clothes back in the basket and place her little stack on top. I'll drop them off in her room later. "Are you hungry?" I say, walking to the fridge. "I was going to make those chicken fajitas you liked for dinner."

"Uh..." she's looking at the pile of her underwear on top of mine, like I think we're some goddamn couple and I'm doing her laundry. *Fuck*

"I mean, I'm going to make chicken fajitas, you're welcome to some."

"Maybe," she says, getting down from the stool. "I might see if Liv and Andy want to go grab something." She takes her clothes off my stack and retreats to the bedroom.

A disappointed breath leaves my lungs. We're roommates, not partners. We're fucking, not dating. We're just two people sharing space...and swapping orgasms.

And I can't let myself forget that.

Chapter 18

Sophie

I'm running out of daylight, but I want to finish the skyline on my current painting. I've been up on this roof almost every day painting, and it feels good. Like finally finding that one puzzle piece that's been staring back at me for days—maybe weeks—and it just clicks into place. I've wanted to invite Liam up here to join me, just to hang out. But that's not what we do.

This is not a relationship. He might have folded my underwear like it was no big deal, and I might be dying to show him my most recent painting. But that's the problem. This isn't what we agreed to. This isn't what he wants.

I pack my brushes and paints back into my grandmother's art box and pause at the door, listening so I don't bump into Cal's neighbor, who always seems to be yelling at someone on her phone. Man, do I feel sorry for whoever her assistant is.

When I'm sure the coast is clear, I go down the stairs, wondering if Liam's home, then chastise myself. He is not my boyfriend, he does not owe me his whereabouts.

When I open the apartment door, I freeze. Liam's leaning against the hallway door, holding my purple vibrator, a wicked smirk tugging at his lips.

"Whatcha doing with that?" I tease, setting down my art supplies.

"I was restocking our condom supply in the bathroom, and you left this in the shower. Am I not leaving you satisfied?"

"You were on a run," I shrug. But the truth was that vibrator couldn't come close to satisfying me the way Liam had over the past three weeks. In fact, the only way I was able to finish in the shower this morning was picturing Liam in there with me. But in my daydream, it wasn't his impressive length that got me to climax...it was imagining him washing my hair. *Shit, this is not good.* This is what I can't let happen. This is just about sex.

"You couldn't wait for me to get home?" Liam muses, smacking the sex toy against his hand.

"What?" I goad him. "You think you can do better than that thing?"

He stalks towards me with a look in his eyes that means I'll soon be utterly satisfied and also unable to walk. But I'm not expecting it when he hauls me over his shoulder and smacks the vibrator against the exposed line of my ass under my cutoffs.

"I think I can do better *with* this thing."

I squeal in delight...until I realize he's taking us to the bedroom.

"No." My voice comes out sharper than I intend, and Liam freezes. I'm having a hard enough time keeping my feelings separate, and the bedroom feels like something I can't take back. I force a low, teasing edge into my voice. "Let's do it right here."

Liam lowers me down his body, searching my face. For a heartbeat, something flickers in his eyes—hurt, maybe—before he grips my waist and lifts me onto the kitchen island.

"It's a good thing you keep this counter so immaculate, I think it's the only surface we haven't christened." He yanks my shorts and underwear off in one motion. "Lean back," he says, tugging me to the edge of the counter and settling himself on the stool.

I lean back on my palms, but I can't tear my eyes off Liam as he turns my vibrator over in his hands. I startle when he hits the power button and the device begins to buzz.

"What do you like to do with this thing?" Liam drags the vibrator across the skin below my belly button, and everything inside me pulls tight. "This?"

"Uh-huh," I breathe out.

"How about here?" He moves the toy up my stomach, scrunching my tank top until he can press the buzzing tip to my already peaked nipples.

"Yeah, that's good."

"Where next, Soph? Where do you touch yourself next?" he asks while drawing lazy circles around each nipple.

"Lower."

He trails the vibrator down against my already sensitized skin, pausing at the crease of my hip, and I writhe on the counter. It's not where I want him, and he knows it.

"Like here?"

"Liam." My voice is a whimper, a plea. I try to rock forward, and he finally complies.

Slowly, he drags it up and down my slit, and I let my head fall back, eyes closing as I sink into the sensation. Liam teases me, pausing at my clit just long enough to nearly tip me over before sliding back down to my entrance and the sensitive skin below. This is what I need. Focus on the sex, lean into the pleasure.

"Look at me, Soph."

I can't. I shouldn't. But I do. I lock eyes with Liam. I might be naked from the waist down, completely exposed to him, but that's not where I feel most vulnerable. That's not what

I'm afraid he'll see when he looks at me like that. I try to clear my mind—of my shower daydream, of lazy mornings in bed, of doing laundry and eating chicken fajitas—and focus on my body, the vibrations, the sensations coursing through my bloodstream.

Not the hunger in his eyes watching the flush creep across my chest.

"Ready for more?" Liam asks, his voice husky, teasing my entrance.

"Don't be gentle," I tell him, spreading my legs wider. I need this to feel this raw and physical. I need to focus on him between my legs, not between my ribs.

"Fuck," Liam grunts, slowly pumping the vibrator in and out. "You're so fucking wet I can see everything, you're so fucking gorgeous."

Liam knows I love his dirty talk. He knows I like it rough, a little raw. He knows how to push all my buttons and to tip me over the edge. But right now, it's not enough.

"You need more, don't you, sweetheart?"

"Yes," I gasp out, even as panic flutters in my chest that the 'more' I'm craving has nothing to do with what he's offering.

He removes the vibrator with a lewd pop and lays it against my stomach so it just rests on my clit. "Hold this," he growls.

The sound of his zipper, the tear of foil, the buzzing on my clit—they all have me so close that when he slams into me, I break. I scream out in pleasure as Liam's cock bottoms out inside me.

"Don't you dare move that vibrator until we're both done," Liam demands between rough strokes. My body starts to contract around him, builds and crashes and builds again until I'm undone, shattered apart in the filthiest, purest way.

"Fuck!" Liam shouts. His body shudders, and he drives into me once, twice, a third time before he drops his head and peppers soft kisses on my jaw and neck. "You're perfect," he murmurs, so quietly I almost miss it.

We are both breathing hard, still connected, when a different vibration causes me to jolt. I glance over at my phone, jumping on the end of the counter.

"Ignore it," Liam says, easing us apart. With his help, I slide off the counter and tug on my shorts.

The ringing stops, then starts again.

What if it's Cal? I've been avoiding all of my family's calls, and my mom's last voicemail threatened to drive to Santa Cruz herself if I didn't answer.

I check the caller ID and let it go to voicemail. The phone beeps, confirming the caller left a message. I stare at my screen. It's probably spam, but then what is this nervous flutter behind my sternum?

"You want to check it?" Liam says softly. I can feel the warmth of his body and the slight brush of his hand on my shoulder.

I hit play on the message.

"Hi, Sophia? This is Vandy Cooper, Senator Langford's assistant. Owen Bishop shared a sample of your work with the Senator, and she would like to know if you're open to a commissioned piece. I wasn't able to find representation listed for you, so I've taken the liberty of sending a proposal directly to your email. Please review it and let me know if you're interested. You can reach me at this number with your answer."

The message ends, and I look up to find Liam's eyes locked on mine.

"Soph," he says, reaching for my waist, then stopping mid-air, his hand dropping to his side. "This is it."

"I don't know, Liam." I hate how small my voice sounds. "I'm not sure I can paint like that anymore."

"Just open the email," he says. He reaches for me again, this time letting his hand settle on my shoulder. The weight steadies me. "I'm right here."

The email from Vandy sits at the top of my inbox, subject line flashing like a neon sign: "Art Commission Proposal." I open it and skim through the details. She wants something similar to my large-scale gallery piece, but in shades of beige.

I suck in a breath when I hit the proposed commission rate.

That fee could change everything. Months of rent covered. Student loan payments caught up. A real fresh start.

Liam waits, holding his breath. His hand lingers on my shoulder, feeding me a steady stream of bravery that I can't seem to muster from within. I turn the phone toward him and watch his eyes widen.

"Holy shit, Soph." Then he's scooping me up in a crushing hug, spinning me around until I laugh out loud. When he sets me down, he doesn't let go, tucking me against his chest. "You did it," he whispers into my hair. "I knew you could."

And I let myself melt into his arms, and suddenly the painting doesn't matter. The money doesn't matter. It's this—his fingers drawing soft lines along my spine, the steady rhythm of his breathing. Fuck if this isn't what I actually want to be chasing.

Everything I swore I wouldn't want from him.

Chapter 19

Liam

"Where the hell are my keys!" Sophie yells, coming out of the bedroom. I scan the breakfast bar, hook her beaded keychain's loop over my finger, and hold it out to her as she frantically tears apart her bag, dumping everything onto the counter.

"Thanks," she says, smiling, as she takes her keys from my outstretched finger. She's wearing my favorite pair of barely there sleep shorts and my Iron Cats hoodie, which I'm pretty sure I'm never getting back. Her curls are a wild mess, and her cheeks still flushed from the newest addition to our morning routine.

"I like that new thing you did with your tongue," she says with a smirk.

"I'll be sure to add it to the rotation." I laugh. Sex with Sophie is so...easy. We instinctively know what will make the other person feel good. When to go harder, and when to slow down. We are in tune with each other, like we have this unspoken connection.

Sophie goes into the kitchen and presses buttons on the espresso machine, sliding a perfect latte across the counter. Over the past week, she's started making me coffee again. I'm not sure if she realizes it, but I do.

Things shifted after she accepted the Senator's commission—nothing profound, no big declarations, but these little things that feel bigger than they should. Our standard couch positions have shifted from opposite ends to her legs draped across my lap. Yesterday, she texted me from the roof to see what she'd painted—the overlook in Pacifica, the cliff, the ocean, and the cypress trees all rendered in muted shades of purple. When I wrapped my arms around her waist from behind and kissed the top of her head, telling her it was beautiful, she sighed and leaned into me. And I never wanted to move.

I'm mid-sip of my perfect latte when Sophie's phone buzzes. "Shit," she mutters, "why does Cal insist on FaceTiming?"

"He likes to see the whites of our eyes," I say.

"Yeah, well, I'm not answering a video call from *his* kitchen. So he'll have to deal with a text saying I'm fine."

"Have you talked to him at all since he left?"

She shakes her head, thumbs tapping across her screen. "I'm sure he means well, but I can't really take his constant disappointment."

"Cal's not disappointed in you, Soph. He's always bragging about you."

"I don't know. Every conversation feels like a checklist of what I'm doing wrong. It's always how I should've stayed in school, or how I can't handle my own money, or how Marshall wasn't good enough—"

"Well, to be fair," I cut in, "that guy sounds like an asshole."

She lets out a huff of agreement, then leans her elbows on the counter and narrows her eyes, studying the still-blank canvas sitting on the easel by the window. It's been almost two weeks since she got the commission, and she hasn't touched it yet. But I know she'll start when she's ready.

"I can hear it in his tone, like I had all this potential and just...wasted it."

Cal's always been proud of Sophie, but I understand how his concern can feel like pressure—because I've felt it too. His constant reminders about contributing to my 401k probably come from love, but they land like judgment.

"I think he wants what's best for you," I say, wishing I had the right words. I wish I could tell her she doesn't have to earn her worth—not for him, not for anyone. To tell her she already is what she's trying so hard to be.

"Maybe," she says, but she doesn't sound convinced. She pushes herself off the counter. "Is it okay if I shower first? I'm meeting Liv and Andy to show them the new exhibit at the de Young."

"Yeah, of course," I say, and I immediately picture her in the shower. This time, I'm imagining myself in there with her—not for sex, but to wash her hair, run my fingers through her scalp, and get those little moans of pleasure from something more than, well, more than what we've been doing.

But that isn't what she wants. She'll let me bend her over the bathroom counter, both of us watching in the mirror as she comes undone, but then she'll push me out the door and shower alone. She'll curl into me after sex and let me trail my fingers over her soft skin, but just before we both doze off, she gets up and rushes to get dressed.

I try not to let it bother me. We agreed to keep this casual. I try not even to look up when she emerges from the shower and heads to Cal's room, wrapped in a towel that barely covers her ass, her curls piled on her head to keep them dry. Okay, so maybe I notice.

Label or not, this is the best thing I've had in a long time—maybe ever—and I don't want to screw it up. I like Sophie. Maybe more than I should. But even if we cut off the sex, I still want to spend time with her. She's smart, funny, unpredictable, brilliant—and somehow my life feels more complete with her in it.

But fuck if I don't want more. I want lazy weekends in our PJs. I want to walk hand in hand with her back from Bar None. I want to bring her flowers for no reason. And I want this to last longer than Cal's house-sitting needs. Which is wild, because I've never wanted any of this domestic shit before. Baseball was always enough—until her.

But she's not looking for a relationship. So I need to get my damn puppy-dog eyes under control and stick to the deal. Even if a part of me still hopes she'll change her mind.

My phone rings.

"Hello?" I say, not recognizing the number.

"Liam Blake? This is William Vallera. I'm not sure if you remember—"

"Coach Bill?" A lump forms in my throat at the sound of my first Little League coach's voice.

I wasn't a bad kid, but I had a lot of energy and misplaced anger. I hadn't hit my growth spurt yet, and I was a little shit when other kids teased me. Coach Bill took me under his wing. He taught me how to use my size-to-strength ratio to my advantage. He made me love baseball and, maybe more importantly, take myself and my talent seriously.

"I guess you do remember me," he laughed. "Listen, I know this is a long shot, but I have some kids in the program right now. Well, they remind me of you." I can almost hear him shaking his head through the phone. "If you're ever in town, maybe you could stop by and show these kids that there is life after their hardships."

My stomach drops. I owe Coach Bill so much, but how could I be some fucking mentor to kids when I failed at the one thing I could do?

"You still there, Liam?" Coach Bill asks when I don't respond.

"Yeah, I'm here. It's just that I don't really...know when I'll be back in town. I'm pretty busy." I feel like an asshole as the lie slips out.

"Of course, I figured as much. But I wanted to reach out. You know I'm proud of you, kid, I talk about you all the time."

"Sure, Coach, thanks." I bite my lip hard to fight the sting behind my eyes.

"Well, keep me in mind if your schedule opens up."

I click the end button on my phone and stare at the blank screen.

"What was that about?" Sophie asks. I'm not sure how long she's been standing in Cal's doorway, listening. She's wearing a baggy pair of jeans and a tight white tank cropped just below her chest, and my eyes linger on the strip of creamy skin exposed at her waist.

"Nothing," I say, lifting my gaze to her face. "Someone wanting a favor."

"Who's Coach Bill?" She crosses her arms over her chest.

"God, Sophie, how long were you eavesdropping on my phone call?" It comes out harsher than I intended. "He was my old Little League coach," I add, trying to soften my tone. "He wanted me to come talk to some kids at the youth center. Sign some balls or some shit. But I'm not going."

Sophie pushes off the doorframe and walks toward me. "Why not?"

"I don't know, I'm just not. I don't have time for that shit."

She glances dramatically around the apartment. "What, you can't squeeze it in between burpees and beers on the couch?"

"Hello pot, meet kettle," I shoot back, but she doesn't rise to the bait.

"Those kids could look up to you. Why won't you go?"

There's something soft in her voice—too soft—and it gets under my skin. I snap.

"Because I'm a fucking failure, Sophie. They don't want to hear from me unless it's as a cautionary tale on how to screw up every aspect of your life spectacularly."

"You're not a failure, Liam." She meets my eyes, and there's something there—something close to pity—and I don't need that. Fuck that.

"Aren't I?" I laugh bitterly. "Look at us. We're both stuck. Stuck in this apartment. Stuck in this life. You got that commission two weeks ago." I jab my finger at the huge blank canvas on the easel in the corner. "And that canvas looks pretty fucking empty."

I instantly want to reel the words back in.

"Wow," she mumbles.

"Soph—" I reach for her, my hand moving almost instinctively, but I stop. Or maybe she does first, stepping just out of reach.

"It's fine," she says, grabbing her bag from the back of the chair. "You clearly want to wallow in your little pity party, so I'll leave you to it."

She strides to the door. Her voice is flat, final. "Enjoy your lonely burpees."

Chapter 20

Sophie

"Oh, you're still letting that hot-as-fuck baseball player steal your bases," Andy says the moment I reach her and Liv outside the de Young.

I try to look confused by her innuendo, but I know my blush gives me away.

"I knew it," Andy chirps as we buy our tickets. "I have excellent just-got-railed radar. I didn't say anything at coffee in case it was a one-time get-it-out-of-our-systems fuck, but this clearly is a thing."

"It's not a thing," I say.

"Oh, it's a thing. I can tell by your glowy skin. Korean ten-step skincare can't hold a candle to regularly getting your banana peeled."

No matter how hard I try to hold back, a laugh still manages to escape.

"Don't encourage her," Liv says, smiling. "But if it's true, spill the details."

"I bet he fucks like he plays baseball," Andy muses as we enter the first exhibit. "Like he knows how to slide headfirst into home base."

Both Liv and I shush her, but we're all giggling like it's a middle school slumber party. Maybe it's been a while since I had girlfriends, because I spill all the details—quietly—as we walk around the museum. I tell them about the first night, when he said he wanted to watch me come, to a few nights ago when he bent me over the couch so we could both still watch the *Survivor* finale.

I hold off telling them about the fight we just had.

"I can't believe you have a sex contract with your brother's best friend," Liv says, taking a sip from her iced coffee from the museum's cafe.

"It's not a sex contract. We just agreed to, you know, blow off some steam together. It doesn't mean anything."

But even as I say this, there's an ache behind my ribs. If this thing with Liam doesn't mean anything, would I care that he isn't going to volunteer at some youth center? If I didn't care, I would have slapped him when he said we were both stuck. But instead, I wanted to curl up in his lap and kiss away the doubt.

Fuck. This was supposed to be friends with benefits, not some Hallmark special: *Washed-up baseball player and burned-out artist show each other the true meaning of love.* This was just sex. Liam has become a friend I care about, but this isn't a relationship, and it certainly isn't love.

I push those thoughts aside as we finish our coffees and head into the main exhibit: Luna Margulies, the whole reason for this trip.

Despite his harsh outburst, Liam was right. My commissioned canvas was still blank in the corner of the living room. I had accepted Senator Langford's proposal and the hefty price tag that came with it, but I had tried to start every day since then...and I just couldn't.

Luna Margulies was my idol. The subject of the critical paper I never finished in grad school. I built my entire final semester around her. I wrote about her, painted like her, tried to channel her. When I saw she had an exhibit at the de Young, I thought her work could unlock whatever had me frozen.

I clear my throat and gesture toward the oversized canvas before us.

"Her work is known for its visceral emotion and bold use of negative space," I say, sounding exactly like the paper I once tried to write. Liv nods, looking between me and the massive piece of art, like I make any damn sense. I don't even believe what I'm saying.

The truth is, I already tried this in grad school. I used to stare at her work for hours, trying to decode it—thinking if I could just crack the formula, I'd unlock something in myself.

But I couldn't. So I quit.

"The art is supposed to make you feel..." I trail off, staring at the individual brush strokes like I'm waiting for the feeling to find me. But it doesn't. And maybe that's the problem. This art doesn't make me feel...anything.

My thoughts drift to Liam. About the way he methodically works through his training routine every morning, keeping his body in peak condition for the game he loves. I think about the way he rattled off stats for every Cubs player since 1987 over three nights at Bar None—not like some cliché sports bro, but like a true student of the game, dissecting the numbers, explaining the strategy, the probabilities behind each play. I remember one time in college when he came home with Cal for Thanksgiving and spent hours on the couch, rewinding the same clip of his swing over and over, analyzing the position of his elbows, his hips, his weight transfer. That spring, he broke the conference record for consecutive hits.

He loved baseball. He still loves it.

I art-docent my way through the rest of the exhibit, explaining the cliché color theory and emotional contrast to Liv and Andy, who nod solemnly and even gasp at all the appropriate moments.

Being here was supposed to remind me of what I wanted to do with my life. I thought that maybe since I'd started painting again, I just needed a little more inspiration. But standing here, I feel nothing. Maybe there's something wrong with me. Maybe I'm just not cut out for this world.

Liam's eyes light up when he talks about baseball, even after being cut. I don't feel that way about any of this anymore.

I don't know if I ever really did.

Chapter 21

Liam

When I hear the keypad beep, I'm on my feet before I even think about it. "Soph," I say, crossing the room as she walks in. My eyes lock onto hers, and I can only hope she sees the regret all over my face. "I'm so sorry about what I said this morning."

"I know," she says quietly, setting down her bag.

I reach for her, then hesitate, my hand hovering before I drag it through my hair instead. I've been replaying our fight all afternoon, and I know I owe her the truth.

"I lashed out because I'm scared of being a washed-up nobody," I say, trying to keep my voice steady. "But I shouldn't have taken that out on you. You have this incredible opportunity with your commission, and I believe in you."

Sophie takes a breath, and I brace for her to tell me off. Instead, she says, "I was wrong to push you. The community center thing is your choice, but don't pretend you don't still love baseball."

I try to interject, but she holds up a hand. "And you weren't wrong about that blank canvas—I do need to do some serious thinking about how to move forward."

She closes the space between us, and I want to pull her the rest of the way to me.

"I know this is casual," she swallows, "but we both care about each other's futures. Maybe it's time we admit that." She reaches up and presses a kiss to my cheek, and something in my chest tightens. "Thank you for being honest with me. You're a good friend."

And for the first time in my life, a woman is saying that to me when I want more.

I want to scoop her into my arms and carry her to the bedroom, to the actual bed—no more of this countertop or yoga mat nonsense. I want to wrap my body around hers, and I want to wake up with hers wrapped around mine.

And more than that, I want to talk about my insecurities and hopes for the future. I want to help her work through whatever's going on with her art. I want to know if she thinks about me when I'm not around, the way I've started thinking about her.

Because this doesn't feel like just friends who happen to care about each other's futures. At least, not on my end. Not anymore.

"Did you make fajitas?" she asks, breaking my train of thought.

"Yeah," I reply with a small laugh. "Yeah, I did. I'll make you a plate."

We sit side by side on the couch, eating our dinner. I think she's going to retreat to Cal's room when we finish, but she suggests we watch a movie instead. She grabs a blanket and tucks herself into my side. I wrap my arm around her and wonder if she can feel my heart beating in my chest. But she lets out a contented sigh and snuggles in.

She barely lasts twenty minutes of the movie before she's sound asleep at my side. I stay that way for a long time, just enjoying the warmth of her steady breathing on my chest. Her little shudders of sleep. I stroke her hair and breathe in the fruity scent of her shampoo. When the movie ends, I do scoop her into my arms. She stirs slightly but then settles back against my chest.

I tuck her into Cal's bed. Kiss her lightly on the temple. And go back to the couch.

"I called Coach Bill," I say when she comes out of the bedroom the next morning. She smiles, her eyes crinkling at the corners, but waits for me to continue. "He wants me to come to the field today at four."

"I think that's a great idea."

"I was wondering..." I glance out the window, thinking how silly this idea is. "If you would come with me? I mean..." I backtrack, "it's totally fine if you're busy. I'm sure you are, and you don't want to—"

"Liam." She smiles, and the knot in my chest loosens. "I'd love to."

Later that afternoon, we pull into the community center parking lot. I swear her little Audi—the one that used to belong to her dad—wasn't made for someone my size. My knees are practically up to my chest, and I can't stop bouncing one of them, nerves rattling around in my chest. Maybe this was a bad idea.

Sophie's hand lands on my knee, and it makes me freeze. "You okay?"

I nod, even though I'm not sure I am, and start tapping my finger against the center console instead.

She parks near the back of the lot, turns toward me in her seat, one leg tucked under her. "We can sit here for a few minutes," she says. "Coach Bill isn't expecting you until four."

Sophie leans back in her seat and starts breathing slow and steady. My finger keeps tapping against the leather, the only outlet for the nerves crawling up my spine. *Tap. Tap. Tap.* She takes another breath, and I'll be damned if I don't mirror it. *Tap. Tap. Tap.* My finger still won't stop.

She reaches across the console, sliding her fingers through mine. I squeeze her hand without thinking, and for the first time all day, my lungs finally fill.

"What if they think I'm a total joke, Soph? What if they look at me and see some washed-up nobody?" I ask, my voice low, but I tighten my grip on her. I want to pull her closer, tuck her under my arm, keep her close. Keep her.

She gives me this little smirk. "What if teenagers think a thirty-year-old isn't cool anymore? I mean, we can basically guarantee that."

"You're not helping," I mutter, but a laugh slips out all the same.

"Look, these kids want someone to look up to. They want someone to take them seriously," Sophie says, her voice steady but soft. "You don't have to promise they'll go pro. You're here to show them that when you pour yourself into something you love, it opens doors."

Her jaw tenses like she hears how hypocritical that sounds, but I don't call her on it.

"You love baseball," she continues. "Baseball gave you purpose. And I believe it still can...it just might not look exactly like it did in high school. Or college. Or even El Paso."

I make a sound that's half laugh, half groan. "Okay. But if they laugh at me, we're out of here."

"Deal," she says, squeezing my hand. Her touch sends a flutter through my entire body that somehow settles my nerves and makes my pulse race at the same time. "I'll be with you the whole time."

Chapter 22

Sophie

The field is absolute chaos when we push through the metal gate. Kids and noise bounce off every surface. I give Liam one more reassuring squeeze before letting our hands drop as I spot an older man approaching.

"Liam Blake," he says, shaking Liam's hand. "You are a sight for sore eyes."

"Thank you for having me, Sir," Liam says, and I'm probably the only one who notices a hint of hesitation in his voice.

"And still as polite as ever. I'm William Vallera." Coach Bill says, extending his hand to me.

"This is Sophie Rhodes," Liam says. "She's..."

"And an old friend of Liam's," I finish, unsure how he was going to introduce me.

"Thank you both for coming. These kids are excited to hear from a real-life baseball player."

"I'm hardly—"

"We brought some balls for Liam to sign." I cut him off, holding out the canvas bag.

"Wonderful, let's head this way." Coach Bill gestures back towards the field.

I place a quick hand on Liam's shoulder. "I'm going to hang back here." I tip my chin toward the metal bleachers. "You'll be fine."

Liam swallows and looks like he's about to protest, but his eyes meet mine, and I nod again, inhaling like we had in the car. "You've got this."

He walks away with Coach Bill, and I find a spot on the metal bleachers. As Liam gets closer, the kids swarm around him. I can't hear what anyone is saying, but I watch as kids tug on Liam's sleeve to get his attention and mime baseball swings. Liam takes his time with each kid, listening to their stories and nodding attentively. Coach Bill steers him towards some older kids taking batting practice in a cage to the left of the infield.

Liam is in his element.

I'd spent nearly every day with Liam for six weeks, and he was no longer the mopey guy from the first days. We'd gone from accidental roommates to convenient sex partners to friends.

We swapped childhood memories and embarrassing stories—like the time he got locked out of his dorm in just a towel and had to shimmy through a window, junk barely covered. I laughed so hard Diet Coke nearly came out my nose, which made him laugh so hard beer actually came out his nose.

We debated everything from launch angle versus contact percentage to the flaws of the gallery system and which parts of *Survivor* are rigged. We also spent countless nights tangled together, memorizing every moan and sigh so we could draw them out again.

We both showed up at Cal's confused, angry, and a little broken, and we both changed.

But watching Liam now, this was different.

He positions himself behind a teen holding a bat. He adjusts his elbow, points to a spot on the horizon, demonstrates how to shift his hips, then cheers wildly when the kid hits the ball hard into the metal fence of the batting cage.

We'd joked about how burned out we were, how disillusioned we felt by the thing that was supposed to bring us ultimate joy. Baseball, like art, was a fickle lover neither of us wanted to keep chasing.

I thought we were the same.

But despite all his earlier nerves, Liam's whole body was radiating joy. His smile, his posture—everything had transformed. I couldn't hide my happiness as I watched him, but I also felt a sharp pang of envy. Yesterday at the de Young, Liv gasped at one of Luna Margullies' most profound pieces, and I caught Andy shedding a little tear at another of her works. And I felt nothing when I was supposed to feel everything.

I push off the metal seat and wander back towards the main building of the community center. My eyes take a moment to adjust to the dimmer light inside the building, and when they do, I see a young girl, maybe around ten, struggling with an armload of art supplies. I rush over to help her unload the basket full of paint and brushes onto the table.

"I'm Talia," she says politely, holding out her hand.

"I'm Sophie," I say, taking her hand for a shake. "What are you working on?" I ask, nodding at the big blank sheet she's unrolling.

Talia sighs, frowning down at it. "I never know what I should paint when it's just...empty. How do I know?"

I hover for a second, then sit on the edge of the table. "I'm...not sure," I admit, then after a breath, I add, "But sometimes it helps to stop thinking about what it *should* be and just...put something down. Anything. Even if it's messy."

Talia studies me for a long moment, then tilts her head. "Are you an artist?"

I let out a shaky laugh, "I...don't know anymore."

Chapter 23

Liam

It's late when I get back to Cal's.

I've spent every afternoon this week at the community center with the kids and Coach Bill. We worked on the kids' swings and their fielding stances, but we also discussed scholarships, internships, and the college application help offered by the community center. I buzz with excitement every night when I get home, but Sophie hasn't come with me since that first afternoon.

That afternoon, I almost didn't go. I told myself it didn't matter—that *I* didn't matter. But Sophie pushed me. She knew the impact I could have on those kids—or maybe the impact they'd have on me. She sees me better than I see myself, knows how much baseball still means to me, even through the anger, the bitterness, the disappointment.

So why can't she see that for herself? And how the hell do I help her see it?

"You look cozy," I say, and toe off my shoes. She's on the couch, curled up under a blanket with a bowl of Froot Loops. She really doesn't eat unless I feed her. I turn towards the kitchen to make her some real food when she pats the couch next to her.

"Come, tell me about your day."

I glance over at the still-blank canvas on the easel by the window. But I don't mention it. I sit down next to her and pull her feet into my lap, digging my thumb into the arch of her foot. She lets out a long sigh, and for everything we've done this summer, this somehow feels like one of our most intimate acts.

"After batting practice," I start, massaging her ankle. "I talked with some of the seniors about opportunities in sports beyond just playing. Things like PR, journalism, and coaching."

"Sounds like a needed pep talk."

I let out a resigned sigh and continue working my hands up her calf.

After we're both quiet for a moment, I ask, "Why did you stop painting?"

She doesn't answer, but she also doesn't stiffen at my direct question. I press my thumb into the ball of her foot, like it's the 'speak' button on a toy. "Not why you dropped out of art school, but why did you quit art?"

She doesn't answer for a long moment, and I worry she's not going to. I'm about to try changing the subject when she finally does

"Art had become something I was supposed to do for other people. Galleries wanted 'Sophia Rhodes'—this image that my professors and mentors had shaped me into. But—" her jaw twitches a little like she's planning what to say next, or maybe figuring it out for the first time. "I think I lost track of who I was underneath all that. Everything I made felt hollow, like I was going through the motions."

"But Soph," I wrap my hand around her calf and pull her across the couch cushions until her legs are draped across my thighs and I can cup her jaw. I'm so lost in the depths of her blue eyes that I almost forget what I want to say. But I drag my eyes away from her and gesture to the skyline painting leaning up against the bookcase. "Your art is stunning."

“I don’t want it to be stunning. I just want it to be me.”

And it’s the realest thing she’s ever said.

She tucks herself into the cradle of my side, and I wrap my arm around her, like I can protect her from her demons.

“I just want to feel something again.” She murmurs into my chest.

I find her chin with my thumb and forefinger and tip her face to mine. I kiss her like I’m trying to memorize her—like I’ll never get another chance.

I want to remind her that she’s capable of feeling everything. Remind her that the little girl who was fearless about her art is still inside this incredible woman, who has been criticized to death—I want to help her find her way back.

She cups my face and kisses me back, like maybe she’ll let me be that for her...just for a while.

I know I’m in trouble. I know I’m in too deep. I know this isn’t what Sophie wants, that I’m not what she wants. But I’m so fucking selfish, or maybe so desperate for this woman, that I’m willing to be anything she’ll let me be for as long as she’ll let me. Especially if it helps her find herself again.

“This summer,” she says, her face buried in my neck, “this time with you. It’s been the most real thing I’ve felt in a long time. Maybe ever.”

I stand with her cradled to my chest and stride towards the bedroom. I think she’s going to protest—about her weight or where we’re headed—but she just grips me tighter. Cal comes home in a few weeks, our clock is ticking, and I don’t want to waste a minute of it.

I hold her in my arms at the foot of the bed and pause—for her to change her mind, to kick me out, to tell me this isn’t what she wants. To say to me she doesn't feel the same way.

“I need you inside me,” she whispers.

You’re already inside me, I think. But I lay her down on the bed and undress her like I’m unwrapping the most precious package.

Her body is so wildly perfect. Like every curve, every valley, every swell was made just for me. I want to memorize the way her lip tilts just before she laughs. The precise way her nose wrinkles when she's concentrating. Or the way her cheeks flush when she's turned on.

The realization that some other guy would get to know all that too...and have her heart, about steals the breath from my lungs.

But Sophie looks up at me with those baby blue eyes and gestures for me to come closer. "Will you hold me?" she asks.

As long as you'll let me.

I slip out of my pants, and I curl onto my side next to her. I pull her tight to my chest, trying to connect our bodies at every point. She tangles her leg around mine.

She tips her face up to mine and takes my face in her hands, then she's kissing me. It's slow and deep, but there's something frantic at the edges, something desperate. I try to pull her closer, to drown out the fear by eliminating the space between our bodies.

"Closer," she whispers, and pushes at my boxers. I shed my underwear and peel hers off her as well until there is nothing but the cool foggy night air coming in the cracked window between us. She curls back into the cage of my arms.

"Please," she says into the skin of my neck. It's not begging—it's permission. And nothing in the world has ever felt more right.

I roll her onto her back and unfold her legs, using my thumb to spread her thighs.

"God, Soph," I say in awe, dropping my forehead to her belly. "This never gets less incredible."

She runs her fingers through my hair, scratching my scalp. I kiss just below her navel, and then the slope of her hip, dragging my teeth lightly across the bone. Her knee tips wider to the side, an invitation. She's pliant and glowing under my touch, and I want to spend the whole night—maybe my entire life—kissing every inch of her.

I drag my tongue slowly up her center, and she's so wet that I can't help the groan that escapes my lips, vibrating her skin. She shifts, but I already know where she wants me. I already know how much pressure she likes. I already know when to bite down in a way that makes her gasp and how to soothe the flick of pain with my tongue. And when she explodes in my mouth, I already know what she tastes like.

I pull back enough to look at her. Her flushed cheeks, the dazed, wrecked look in her eyes. She's barely stopped convulsing when she's pulling at my shoulders, trying to wiggle down further underneath me.

"More," she breathes.

And I don't waste another second giving her what she wants. I roll the condom on and position myself between her thighs.

We've done this enough times that her body opens to me easily now, like it's welcoming me home. Still, I go slow and reach between our bodies to stroke her.

She runs her nails up and down my back, over the plane of my shoulder blade, before digging her fingers into my hip and pulling me into her.

I need you inside me, echoes around my head.

I bend her knee, push her leg up, and press into her. She gasps and sighs and whimpers, and I fold over her to catch every moan with my mouth. I'm fully seated now, deep in this position, and the sensation of her stretching around me is almost enough for me to erupt right there. I take a deep breath and vow to take my time, to make this last. I move my hips slowly, deliberately, pressing deep, so fucking deep. She arches into me like we're made for this, and maybe we are. Maybe I was made for her.

"Yes, Liam," she gasps, and I can't hold back. I drive into her with the exact force I know she likes. She cries out, and then we are both coming, hard and fast and messy and perfect.

I collapse on top of her and roll us both to the side so I don't crush her. She curls right back into my chest, and I pull her tight. Both of us are breathing heavily, labored. I stroke her hair and kiss her temple.

"Liam." There's a tremble in her voice when she whispers my name, but also a contentment, a promise, and I swear I'll spend the rest of my life chasing that sound. "Stay."

And I know I'll never leave.

This bed, this apartment, this heart.

Chapter 24

Sophie

I think I'm falling for him.

Who am I kidding—I've already fallen, hard. Liam gets me in a way no one ever has. He never asks me to be more or less than I am. He knows where I left my keys and how to unlock the pleasure in my body. He understands the difference between my frustrated sighs and the sharp gasp of a yes—and he knows how to respond to both. He knows when to push and when to hold space.

But more than anything, he understands how crushing it is to carry the weight of other people's expectations.

He doesn't see *Sophie*, Cal's kid sister. Or *Sophia*, the artist with something to prove.

He just sees me.

I've already started imagining what could come next. For so long, my future felt pre-written—like I'd boarded a train years ago and never questioned where it was headed. Then I abruptly got off, and I've been stuck at this station for the last two years.

With Liam, everything feels different. I'm still unsure what the future holds for me or where art or my career fits into it, but for the first time, not knowing doesn't feel like I'm lost or stuck—it feels expansive. And I think that is because I don't have to do it alone. My future, our future, can be shaped by us.

Maybe when Cal comes home, Liam and I don't have to let this go. Maybe this could be something more.

I turn under the grounding weight of his arm and bury my face in his chest, in his scent, citrus and musky and safe. I tuck myself tighter against his body like I'm trying to cocoon into his flesh.

He responds, just a sleepy pull that brings me closer. His arm curls around my back, pressing me to him like he's anchoring us both. His eyes stay closed, but I know he's awake—barely. Like we're both suspended in the softness of a dream we don't want to leave.

"I could get used to this," he whispers into my hair.

"Same."

"Yeah?" he pulls back to look into my eyes, and I nod. "I'd like that."

"So would I," I agree and nuzzle into his body.

He tucks my leg over his hip, his hand tracing slow, aimless paths along my thigh. His phone buzzes on the nightstand, and we both freeze. He glances over. "It's not Cal," he confirms before pulling me tighter to his body, almost possessive. One hand squeezes my calf in a rhythm that feels more instinct than thought, and he presses a kiss into my hair. I could stay here all day, maybe never leave this bed, these arms, ever.

His phone buzzes again.

"Fuck me," he mutters and snakes a hand out to grab it. I try to shift away, give him space, but he holds me tight against him. "Yeah," he says into the phone, his other hand trailing up the ridges of my spine.

"Jackson, wait—start over," he says, sitting up and pulling me with him until I'm nearly in his lap. I glance up at his face, trying to read his dazed expression. Is it good news? Bad?

"It's July fucking 30th. You've got to be kidding me," he mutters, before easing me onto the bed and striding to the window in his underwear. I tuck the sheet around my nearly naked body and wait, an uneasy lump rising in my throat.

"Yeah, yeah, of course," he says, nodding his head, then scrubs his hand through his hair. His eyes flick to mine for a moment, then he looks away, like he can't hold my gaze. "No, of course...this is great. Yeah, I'll be there."

He drops his hand and turns to look at me. His mouth opens like he's about to say something, but nothing comes out. He paces in a tight circle, rubbing the back of his neck. For a second, he just stands there, staring at the floor, then he lifts his head.

"I got a roster spot," he says, still sounding dazed. "Sophie—it's the Cubs' Triple-A team. In Iowa. My agent said they need someone with utility experience and a solid bat. I report tomorrow."

My throat goes dry.

I should be happy for him, thrilled, but instead the last seven weeks play like a bad highlight reel through my mind. He was never done with baseball. Of course, he wasn't. He'd kept up his brutal training routine, his disciplined diet, still breaking down swing analytics over our morning lattes.

While I was staring at a blank canvas and a dwindling bank account.

I'd never ask him to give up his dream, but all I can think of is how cruel the timing feels. We just found each other—really found each other. For the first time in years, something in my life felt right. And now he's leaving.

This summer—just like he said—was a break. A pause on the path to the dream he never gave up on.

The one that takes him away from me just when I thought we had a future.

"You're leaving?" I ask, and I hate how small my voice sounds.

"It's the Iowa Cubs," he says. "Their starting utility guy pulled a hamstring—he was batting .312. If I can show I've still got my swing, it's my best shot."

"But you're leaving...tomorrow?"

He exhales, and his shoulders slump. "I have to go, Soph. I mean...this was always the goal."

He won't even look at me when he says it.

Of course it was.

I was just a detour.

Just sex. No strings. Just like we'd said.

Then why did it hurt so much?

I watch his back. The ridges of muscles shift as he breathes, looking out the bedroom window to the street below. I thought we'd become friends this summer. I thought we'd become more.

He turns around to look at me, his eyes searching mine, panicked and desperate. A true friend would push down the hurt, the petty jealousy in my gut, and celebrate the one thing he's wanted his entire life.

But I can't.

I gather my things, and before I slip out of the room, I whisper, "We were supposed to be broken together."

Chapter 25

Liam

I always thought the top would feel more dramatic. Turns out, it smells like a warm locker room and a broken heart.

Chapter 26

Sophie

I park in the same spot at the back as when I came to the community center with Liam. God—was that already two weeks ago?

He'd called a few times, but I didn't answer. It was easier—for both of us. He needed to focus on baseball, not get sucked into my wallowing. Besides, we had agreed that whatever it was between us was just for the time Cal was away. Cal was coming home tomorrow, so the expiration date was up. No need to complicate things when he had his future to focus on.

Liam was moving on, and I was still stuck.

"Thank you for coming," Angelica, the director of the art program, says, holding out her hand when I walk through the glass double doors. "I know you said you couldn't commit to a teaching position here full-time, but we appreciate you filling in until we find someone. The kids will be thrilled to have a professional artist to learn from."

"Oh, I'm hardly a..." I start, but I think about Liam. He showed up here for weeks for these kids. And he was still a baseball player—being released didn't change that fundamental part of who he is. "Thank you for having me."

"Kids," Angelica says as we enter the room. Children of varying ages are seated at long tables, each with colored pencils and pots of paint. "This is Sophia Rhodes. She's an artist."

For the first time in years, I don't flinch at the title.

After discussing color and art for about ten minutes, I let the kids loose to work on their creations. I circle the room, looking at the kids' painted flowers and hand-sketched superheroes.

I circle the tables until I come to the last table in the back corner of the room. I recognize the young girl sitting there. "Talia, right?" I say. She nods, but she looks uncomfortable. I glance at her paper. It's blank.

I slide into the seat next to her. "Tell me about your art."

"There isn't any," she says and flips her paper over.

I nod, but stay silent. Waiting.

"I want to paint a sunset."

"Sunsets are beautiful."

"But I want to use these colors," she drags her hand around a cluster of paint jars in front of her. Cerulean, teals, Aegean Blue, Celadon, and a bottle of the most vibrant neon pink. "But Katelyn says these aren't sunset colors."

"Close your eyes, Talia," I say. "Can you see your sunset?"

"Uh-huh," she nods, eyes squeezed tight.

"Then those are sunset colors. No one else can tell you what art is to you."

She opens her wide eyes and looks at me, still unsure.

"The artist makes the art. And you're the artist, Talia. You're not here to make the 'right' kind of art. You're here to make *your* art."

She's tentative at first, but then she grins and reaches for the brightest green paint in her pile—the perfect green for a sunset.

I watch her paint with complete confidence, using colors that feel right to her, rather than what she's been told they should be. And I think about my own blank canvas back at Cal's apartment. The Senator's commission sits there, waiting for me to paint what she expects instead of what wants to come out of me.

The artist makes the art.

Maybe the problem isn't that I can't paint the commission. Maybe the problem is that I'm trying to paint someone else's vision instead of my own.

I know what I have to do.

I have to turn down the commission.

Chapter 27
Sophie

When I walk into the apartment that evening, I almost burst into tears at the sight of my big brother sprawled out on the couch.

"Cal," I say, a tremble in my voice.

"Smudge?" Cal stands from the couch, using his nickname for me, which I had hated throughout my childhood, but now feels like a warm blanket. "What are you doing here?"

I let him wrap me in his arms, and I bury my nose in his shirt. He smells like the cologne our dad used to wear.

"I left Marshall. You said I could always come here." I decided to go back to the reason I initially showed up here, despite a lot of other things happening in the last ten weeks.

"Of course," he says, rubbing big circles on my back. "I'm glad you came."

He pulls back and holds me by the shoulders like he's studying me for bruises.

"I'm fine, Cal."

The bruises are all on my heart.

Cal tips his chin to my painting on the easel. Before Liam left, he swapped out my blank canvas for the San Francisco skyline I'd painted that very first morning on the roof. It was like he was trying to remind me I was more than a blank canvas.

"You're painting again," Cal says.

"Not really," I say. "It was just to pass the time this summer until I figured out what's next. None of it was...real."

Cal watches me for a long beat. "Are we still talking about that skyline painting?"

I look away and blink back the tears that are threatening to break free.

Cal pulls me back into the hug he knows I need and shushes me gently.

"I'm glad you finally left Mr. Artsy McDouchebag," he says.

I freeze. That was what Liam had called him.

He knows. Of course, he knows.

I pull back from his arms and bite my lip, trying to decide which way I want to spin this lie. But he doesn't let me.

"I saw Mr. Snowflake in the background of my bedroom the first time I FaceTimed Liam," he says with a knowing laugh. "No one else still has that same dingy stuffed animal from their childhood."

"But if you knew we were both here, why didn't you say anything?"

"It seemed like maybe you both had a lot to figure out first. You didn't need me butting in."

"Cal Rhodes not butting in with advice? That seems wildly out of character," I joke, but I can't believe how much relief I feel.

"Call it growth," he chuckles and squeezes my arm.

"Have you..." I swallow down the knot forming in my throat. "...talked to him?"

"Yeah," Cal nods. "I called when I got back to the States, during my layover in Dallas. He told me he was in Iowa. And he told me you were here. Instantly confessed you'd both been here together."

"And you didn't threaten to fly to Iowa to punch him in the face?"

"Nah, I'd break my hand on that square jaw of his."

I huffed a little laugh, turning away and wiping my eyes.

"Soph, is that honestly what you think?" He reaches out to squeeze my shoulder. "You know I've only ever wanted you to be happy."

"I know. But sometimes your advice sounds like you don't trust me to know what's best for me."

Cal's quiet for a beat. "That's fair. And actually, that's exactly what Liam said—that you already know who you are, even if I can't see it yet."

I cross my arms, pretending I'm not melting inside over Liam defending me to my brother.

"So are you two...?" Cal settles himself on one of the stools, waiting.

I shake my head. "It was just a thing."

"I've known Liam Blake almost my entire life," he says. "He doesn't do anything half-assed. God love him, but he doesn't start things he's not serious about."

He waits for me to reply, but I can't quite form words. My thoughts spiral back through the summer—egg sandwiches waiting for me every morning, him always knowing exactly where I'd dropped my keys. The way he started buying almond milk without me asking, how he'd wordlessly hand me a sweatshirt before opening windows. All those tiny gestures I'd ignored suddenly feel like the gentlest way someone could say "I care about you" without ever saying the words.

"I've known you your *entire* life, Smudge," he goes on. "You don't half-ass anything either. But you also don't always ask for what you want. You tend to say what you think others want. Like that time you told Mom you wanted tacos for your birthday dinner—even though they're Dad's and my favorite, not yours."

He nods at the painting over my shoulder. "Or saying that's not real art because some pretentious professor decided your abstracts were more emotionally complex."

I look away, but he's not done.

"Or suggesting a fling to a guy you really care about because you couldn't believe he could want the same thing."

"But we agreed," I mumble, but it sounds weak even to my own ears.

"You can try to tell yourself that you don't matter to him, but I'll tell you this, when I saw Mr. Snowflake, I knew you were here. But it was when I saw the look of fury on Liam's face when I suggested whoever he had here didn't matter to him, that I knew it was real."

My mind buzzes with everything Cal just said. I can't seem to process it all—that maybe what I was feeling, he really was feeling too. That maybe I could trust myself enough to ask for what I want.

My eyes flick up to my painting—the skyline suddenly seeming to represent so much more. To me. To us. To what we were starting, even if we both were too scared or stubborn to admit it.

I told Talia that the artist creates the art, not the other way around. I had been ready to turn down Senator Langford's commission, to tell her I couldn't create what she wanted. But I suddenly had another idea.

I opened the text thread between the Senator's assistant, Vandy, and me. I explained I had a new direction for the Senator's piece, one that would more accurately represent who I was as an artist and, I think, the vision she wanted for the art in her home. I sent the picture of the skyline, along with a few other things I had painted this summer. The art that came out of the magical summer with Liam, when I stopped trying to be what everyone else expected and just let myself feel. The stuff I created when I felt truly inspired to paint for myself.

I hit send on my new idea.

If she hates it, that's okay. At least I know I was honest.

As soon as I send it, my first instinct is to text Liam. I know he'd be so proud that I'm finally following my heart as an artist, that I found the courage to be authentic. But that would be hypocritical. When he got that call—his dream opportunity—I should have celebrated with him. I should have told him how proud I was, how much he deserved it. Instead, I let my own fear turn his victory into my loss.

"I think I fucked it up, Cal."

"The good news is sometimes you get a second chance at a dream you thought was over." He pulls two tickets from his back pocket and slides them across the breakfast bar. "I have an extra ticket to the Giants-Cubs game tonight." He taps the ticket. "In the family section. Any interest?"

My eyes flick to him, going wide with disbelief.

"He got called up, Soph," he says, with a little lopsided smile. "He made it to The Show."

Chapter 28

Liam

"Okay, Giants fans, we don't normally cheer for the opposing team, but let's make an exception for San Francisco's own, Liam Blake, at his first at bat in the big leagues for the Chicago Cubs."

I can hardly believe Mike Krukow just said my name.

I try to swallow my nerves as what sounds like the entirety of Oracle Park seems to be cheering...for me.

Everything about the last three weeks has been surreal. I'd hardly gotten my paperwork signed in Iowa, passed my physical, and taken a few days of batting practice, when I started in a triple-A game against the Toledo Mud Hens. We won. After the game, the coach said, "Nice work tonight, Blake. Too bad we won't get to keep you with us." I thought I was getting cut again, that my second chance was just a few long plane rides and triple RBI.

But I can't lie, the first thing I thought was that I could go back to Sophie. That I could try to convince her we were more than friends with benefits, more than a summer fling. To try to tell her I had wanted more from the day we woke up in Cal's bed together, but I was too stubborn or scared to admit it. Then my coach continued. "Do that same thing at the plate in San Francisco tomorrow."

So here I am. In a Cubs uniform, in a Major League Baseball park, taking a few practice swings, trying to delay walking to the plate for as long as I could.

"You've got this, Blake," the batting coach says from the dugout. I walk onto the diamond and glance up at the stands, but the stadium lights blind me from seeing anything. I know my mom is up there. And I'd sent a ticket to Coach Bill. Cal and his parents, too. He and I talked a few days ago. I confessed everything before he'd even said hello. He just laughed and said, "It's about fucking time you two realized you're perfect for each other."

But it was too late.

I hadn't told Sophie how I felt—instead, I told her I had to leave. I'd tried to call her a million times in the past three weeks, but her avoidance was pretty clear. Whatever I felt, whatever *more* I wanted for us, was not what she wanted. She was clear from the beginning; no one gets attached.

I'm the idiot who did.

"Now up to bat for the Chicago Cubs, Liam Blake."

The crowd goes wild.

The camera on the cable system zips past as I step up to the batter's box. I wonder if she's watching from home? Had Cal told her?

I knew she cared. I had to believe she did. Maybe she didn't want more than sex, but all those nights we stayed up just talking, holding each other. All those quiet mornings drinking coffee or the chatty walks home from Bar None.

I knock my cleats with my bat and kiss my fist—something I'd been doing since high school after I saw an MLB player do it—and step into the box.

The pitcher's first pitch whizzes past me.

"Strike one!" the ump calls from behind me, and my pulse speeds up. I need to get my head in the game.

The next ball sails a little outside.

"Ball!"

I take a deep breath. Sophie's face flashes in my mind—her coy smile, those bouncy curls, the way she believes in me. And right then, I decide: no matter what happens, no matter how she responds, I'm going to tell her exactly how I feel. I'm going to tell her I love her.

The pitcher narrows his eyes and lets the ball fly.

I know it's my pitch—the one I've been waiting for my whole life. My chance to swing for the fences.

Crack.

I make my way to the players' parking lot. It's hours after the game. Hours after my first big league home run. Hours after we won. After I showered off the champagne the guys sprayed me with in the locker room. And after I asked Cal to take my mom home, so I could use her car. The team flies out tomorrow afternoon, and I have something I need to do before we leave for Cincinnati.

But as I walk towards the old Civic, someone is sitting on the hood of the car—someone with bouncy curls and perfect curves and the biggest smile.

"Soph?" I say, but I'm already running towards her.

She jumps off the car and launches herself into my arms.

"Liam," she gasps as I spin her off the ground. "I'm so proud of you, and I should have told you that three weeks ago, and I am so fucking sorry. You deserve all of this. And I don't care if you won tonight or ever, but oh my god you hit a home run and..."

I cut her off with a kiss.

She melts into my arms and kisses me back. For a long moment, we are just lost in each other, but then she pushes against my chest and I reluctantly separate.

"What is this?" I ask, as I take in her Cubs jersey over my favorite cut-off shorts. She spins around to reveal my name spelled out in hand-glued rhinestones, with hearts on either side, on the back of the jersey.

"I needed something to wear to your game."

"You were in the stands?" I ask.

"Of course, the whole time," she says, and I pull her mouth back to mine.

"Stop distracting me," she says, pulling back. "I need to tell you something."

I might take my lips off her, but I refuse to let her go. I keep my hands banded around her lower back. She tips her head back to look up at me.

"I've spent most of my life doing what I thought others expected of me, being who others wanted me to be. Until I didn't know what I wanted for myself, I thought that made me broken."

"You could never be broken," I rush to assure her.

"I know." She places her hand on my chest. "Because you helped me figure that out this summer. You helped me find my way back to myself."

"I wouldn't be here with you either, Soph. You got us out of the house, you got me to the community center. You made me take myself seriously again."

"I think that's the whole point." She inhales and exhales like it's the first full breath she's taken in weeks. "I like me better when I'm with you. I don't want to be broken together. I want to be whole...next to you."

"Oh, Sophie. I want that more than anything. I'm sorry I didn't tell you that sooner. I'd give it all up if I had to."

"God, Liam, no, that's what I mean. We contain multitudes. You're a baseball player, a mentor, and a guy who's oddly good at math and a million other things that make you you. I want all of them. I'm a latte-making, counter-scrubbing artist who's learning to be a teacher so the next generation of artists doesn't have to feel the way I felt. And I want to be all these things with you."

"You're an artist?" I ask, but I can't hide my smile.

"I am," she says confidently, but then that confidence dips for a moment. "But there's one more thing I'd like to add to that list. I'd like to be your girlfriend."

I want to tell her no, that girlfriend isn't enough for what I want. But we have time for that, for all that.

"I'd like to be your boyfriend."

"I think I love you, Liam Blake."

"Oh, Sophie. I know I love you. And I want to spend the rest of my life showing you."

I take her in my arms and spin her into a low dip, then kiss her deeply and thoroughly. I can still hear the crowd going wild in my head.

I really did knock it out of the park.

Epilogue

Sophie

I'm waiting in the players' parking lot, sitting on the hood of my old Audi, wearing my Cubs jersey—the official one with Blake embroidered across the back. After Liam finished last season, the Cubs signed him to a one-year contract. And Liam is thrilled.

He's already in talks with KNBR about joining their commentating team when his current contract expires—or staying on with the team as a batting coach. Or whatever else comes next for him. Whatever opportunity it may be, it will be a move forward.

We spent the off-season setting up our home together—a little understated cottage in Pacifica. Even a year and a half's baseball salary meant we could have gotten something bigger, something flashier, but this place is perfect for us. It has a small but lovely kitchen, and Cal bought us a fancy espresso machine as a housewarming gift, which Liam still can't use. Liam started a garden in the back and fixed up the small shed into my artist's studio.

It's close to his mom and my parents, as well as the community center where we both still volunteer. Liam works with the teens and Coach Bill whenever he's in town, and I teach a weekly children's art class. That is, between working on the steady flow of commission requests.

Senator Langford loved the new concept I pitched to her. She said the skyline reminded her of growing up in the Bay Area, and she wholeheartedly wanted me to continue the commission with my vision. After she mentioned my art during her book tour and emphasized the importance of supporting artists, requests started pouring in. However, I only say yes to the ones that truly inspire me —the ones I genuinely want to do.

"Is that major league baseball phenom, Liam Blake? Fresh off another win?" I say when Liam walks into the parking lot, bag slung over his shoulder.

"I'd hardly call it a phenom, more like a thirty-two-year-old utility player with a bum knee," he says, but he's smiling proudly. "Is that artist Sophia Rhodes, whom the San Francisco Chronicle recently named 'one to watch in the SF art scene'?" he adds, kissing me as he steps between the V of my legs.

"Just Sophie is fine," I say, kissing him back. "Should I feel guilty for not feeling bad that the Giants lost?"

"Nah, even I feel a little guilty," he adds, slinging his bag into the back seat. "Let's get out of here." He's off for three days before he has to meet the team in the next city. And we already plan on spending the entire time tangled around each other in our bed.

But I have another idea first.

"I think we should celebrate your win here, Mr. Blake," I say, tipping my head toward the back seat. Liam had shared a dream he'd had in those early days at Cal's about me and the backseat after a win, and I planned on making that dream come true tonight. And as many times as I can this season.

"You're already a fucking dream come true," he laughs, scooping me into his arms and opening the door.

I always thought love would feel more dramatic. Turns out, it just feels like finally being me.

Thank You!

Thank you so much for reading this novella. If you liked it, please consider leaving a review on Amazon, Goodreads or your own socials. Please tag me @ajclaremontwrites.

And if you want sneak peeks, bonus chapters, and behind-the-scenes on my writing journey, subscribe to my newsletter at www.ajclaremont.com

More in the Across the Hall Series

Faking It (Out Now!)
Kiss & Break Up (Spring 2026)
Sleep On It (Summer 2026)
Off the Market (TBD)

Sneak Peek!

Want more from the residents Across the Hall?

Wondering how Liv and Owen ended up engaged?

Check out Book 1:
Faking It

Available now!

A charming stranger turns pretend fiancé.
It was supposed to be one fake date.
They seemed to forget they're *Faking It*.

And Stay Tuned for Book 3:
Kiss & Break Up

Coming Spring, 2026
One wild night. No names.
Now he's her new assistant.
They've already hooked up...now they have to *Kiss and Break Up*.

...Turn the page for a sneak peek!

Chapter 1

Harper

Fuck work, fuck this fucking job, and fuck Milo for thinking I can't do this on my own. In fact—fuck all men.

I shoot the whiskey Frankie, the bartender, just filled and slam the glass down on the sticky bar with a little more force than needed. Frankie quirks a brow.

Except Frankie. He's cool. Frankie is actively helping me get drunk.

I don't really mean fuck Milo either. He's my best friend and business partner, and he already knows everything about me, including how to put up with all my shit. He's been my ride-or-die since we ditched toxic corporate hospitality to build something better together.

He's the only person I trust with both my career and my secrets.

Which is exactly why he should have known better than to hire me an assistant. Another man thinking he knows what's best for me. I know he means well. He always does. But fuck him for thinking I need a goddamn assistant. He doesn't have one.

Because I have boundaries, Harper, he'd said. Translation: he can leave the office at a decent hour and I can't. So clearly I need someone to do my job for me. So he hired some imbecile to what...get me coffee and make photocopies or some bullshit? It's 2026. We don't even *need* photocopies. What is this kid going to do besides follow me around all day and get in my way?

I work better alone.

I throw back the rest of the whiskey and lift my hand to Frankie for a refill. Then squint at Milo's text from earlier with the name and resume of whoever this guy is.

Sullivan M. Bennett.

I don't bother opening the attachment Milo sent. I don't need to. Who names their kid Sullivan anyway?

My head is starting to throb, but I'm not quite ready to sulk back to my apartment. It's only 11 p.m. That would be the earliest I've been home in months, all because Milo said that if I didn't leave the office, he'd have his husband Parker, who's built like a linebacker, come and physically carry me home.

So I left.

Not because he told me to.

But because I wanted to stop at Bar None.

"Whiskey, neat," a voice says beside me.

I hadn't noticed anyone take the barstool next to mine. Certainly not anyone with a voice like caramel, or tiny flecks of stubble shadowing an angular jaw.

He catches me staring and lifts his glass, tipping his chin in a silent toast before taking a sip.

I don't raise my glass, but I drink anyway, eyes forward.

"Celebrating?" he asks, "or commiserating?"

The question is casual. The voice is not.

It slides low in my belly and settles there, unexpected and entirely distracting.

"Sorry," he says, pushing up from the bar. "I didn't mean that to be weird. I'll leave you to it."

He picks up his glass and wipes at a ring of condensation on the bar with his cocktail napkin before turning away without a backward glance.

"Maybe both," I say. There's something that makes me want him to stay. And before my brain catches up with my mouth, I add, "You don't have to go."

He turns back with a sheepish smile, avoiding my eyes. His hair, a warm brown, is messy in a way that looks unintentional, and the laugh lines around his eyes suggest he's older than me, but not by much. He sets his whiskey glass down on the bar but doesn't let go of it. Doesn't sit. When he finally looks at me, his eyes are warm, a deep shade of amber—but there's a hint of something underneath. Concern, maybe. Like he's bracing for something he didn't plan on.

"What about you?" I gesture to the barstool beside me. "Celebrating or commiserating?"

I don't hit on men in bars. Hell, I don't even talk to men in bars. I've learned that one polite hello can turn into a man bun explaining the weather to me or a tech bro telling me I should smile more.

But something about this guy makes me want to—I don't know.

Talk.

"Maybe both," he echoes, his tentative smile tilting a little.

And that voice ripples straight down my spine.

I'm suddenly thinking about more than conversation.

"So what are you celebrating or commiserating?" he asks, dragging my attention away from the way his forearm flexes when he swirls his whiskey glass.

"Oh," I hesitate. I'm celebrating Milo and I securing our largest client project to date, and I'm commiserating that he doesn't think I can handle it alone. But I don't want to talk about work right now. I talk about and think about work twenty-three and a half hours a day. It's usually the only thing that holds my attention.

"Just work," I finish.

Except right now.

I meet his eyes. "What about you?"

"I agreed to do a favor for an old friend," he says, sliding onto the stool.

"That's nice of you." My body angles toward his like a magnet. "I'm sure your friend appreciates it."

"He does," he says, finishing his drink in one gulp, "I'm just a little unsure if I'm up for it, you know."

His words feel broken somehow. Lived in. I take the last sip of my drink and wave to Frankie.

"You can put them both on my tab, Frankie," I say as the bartender refills our glasses. "We're celebrating."

"Congratulations," Frankie says, finishing his pour with the disinterest of a bartender who has seen too much.

"To drowning our sorrows and better tomorrows," I toast with my dad's favorite saying, and he clinks my glass with a slight chuckle. We both take long sips of our whiskey, and the alcohol, or maybe his gentle smile, loosens a knot inside my chest that I had presumed was necessary for my body to operate.

He watches me over the rim of his glass. "Bad day?"

"Bad day," I confirm. "You?"

"Bad year," he says, and there's something in his voice that makes me look closer. "Figured whiskey and people-watching might help."

"Is it helping?"

"Yeah," he says, meeting my eyes. "Actually, it is."

We fall into easy conversation after that. Not first date bullshit, but like we are on our twelfth date or twelve hundredth, like we already know all the little details, and now it's just stories and half-finished thoughts. Connection and laughter that sneaks up on me, relief of not being Harper-who-has-it-all-handled for once. Time slides by, marked only by empty glasses and the way I keep leaning a little closer without meaning to.

"Hey," he says eventually. "I have to use the restroom." He hitches a thumb over his shoulder, then hesitates. "Will you still be here, or do you need to head out?"

"No," I laugh. "It's way too early for me to go home. The neighbors wouldn't know what to think if I showed up before midnight."

"Ah." He nods, and I have the sudden, irrational urge to swim in the warm gold of his eyes when he smiles. "I used to be a night owl, too, but this is the latest I've stayed up in months."

"Maybe I should let you get to bed." And I'm pretty sure I'm smirking.

He goes quiet for a beat, studying me—or maybe choosing his next words. I hold my breath.

I don't want him to go.

"This has been well worth ruining my sleep score on my RootDown app."

Heat rushes up my neck. It's the way he's looking at me, appreciation edged with something darker, something that slides down my spine like melted chocolate.

"My business partner is obsessed with that app too," I say, forcing a lightness to my voice. "Go." I tip my chin toward the back hallway. "I'll order us another round."

He hesitates, then smiles before heading off.

I flag Frankie down, order another whiskey I absolutely don't need, and tell myself I should absolutely stay seated right here on my barstool.

That I should let this be a pleasant conversation and nothing more.

But my feet are already heading toward the bathroom hall.

When he steps out of the bathroom, he startles at the sight of me leaning against the opposite wall.

He recovers quickly, holding the door open behind him. My heart is hammering hard enough that I'm sure he can hear it echoing down the narrow hallway.

For half a second, I think about walking past him. Splashing cold water on my face. Resetting. But my head—usually crowded with deadlines and menu tests and overhead projections—won't think about anything but him.

I hook my finger into his belt loop and tug.

He looks down, confused for exactly one beat, then lets me guide him backward into the small bathroom. I reach behind him to twist the lock, the click loud in the quiet space. I'm close enough to feel the heat of him, close enough to hear when his breath hitches.

"I've never really..." he pauses, swallows. "I don't usually—"

I quiet him with my mouth.

His lips are warm and taste like whiskey—his or mine, I can't tell—and his hand slides around my waist. I deepen the kiss, and he responds immediately, stepping closer, backing me up until the counter digs into my hip.

"You taste incredible." He kisses down my neck to my exposed collarbone. I rise on my toes to give him better access. He hoists me onto the counter and steps between my legs, my skirt hiking up, exposing bare thighs. He lets out an appreciative sigh.

I twist my hands in his shirt and drag him closer. His chest is solid beneath my fingertips, his pulse pounding hard and fast, matching mine. We kiss until my lips feel bruised, but it's not enough. I reach for the button of his jeans, and he pulls back, just a millimeter from my lips.

"I live close by, do you want to—" he starts, then his mouth finds mine again. His hands slide up my thighs, thumbs pressing into the inside of my legs, close enough to send sparks across my skin, but not close enough.

I live nearby, too. A few blocks. But I'm already too close to combustion to leave. Besides, if we stop now, I might come to my senses. Start thinking.

And right now, I don't want the part of my brain that runs ten steps ahead, calculating outcomes and spotting missteps. I want the small, neglected part that just wants to feel good. To focus on his hand gripping my thigh, almost possessively, while the other slips beneath my sweater for the first time.

"I don't want to leave," I breathe when his thumb grazes my nipple. "I want this. Now."

"God, you feel incredible," he murmurs against my neck as his hand slides up my thigh. His grip is firm, thumbs digging into my legs, close enough to make me ache. "I want to touch you more."

"Do it." I rock my hips forward to meet his hand.

His thumb drags upward, and he lets out a breathless curse when he realizes how wet I am for him.

"Yes," I gasp, pulling his mouth back to mine as his thumb slips beneath the elastic of my underwear. He strokes slowly at first, then with purpose, until he finds a rhythm that makes my whole body tense. I writhe against the counter as he circles my clit with steady, deliberate pressure, and I can feel myself tightening almost immediately.

"That's right, sweetheart."

When I'm about to beg for more, he slides two fingers inside me.

The sensation is shocking and exactly what I want, and I shatter. My breath catches as the orgasm crashes through me, fast and overwhelming, my body convulsing as it takes over completely. He doesn't pull away. He keeps the same rhythm, guiding me through with soft praises—*that's right, I've got you*—until I'm trembling and boneless against him.

I can't speak. I can barely move. But I need my mouth on his again.

"I'm Max," he stammers between my desperate kisses. "I never—we never—"

I fumble for his zipper, desperate to touch him now.

"Fuck," he groans when I slide my hand into his jeans. He's already hard. I squeeze him once, desperate to feel more of him.

"Do you have a condom?" I say, scooting to the edge of the counter.

"Oh. Yeah. I think—" he grits out, my hand moving rougher now. "But do you—are you sure?"

The familiar buzz of my phone makes my hand falter. He stills.

"Shit." I pull my hand free, and reality slams back.

"It's okay," he rushes. "I'm sorry. We don't have to do anything."

"No," I say, hopping down from the counter and reaching for my bag. "You were great." The words come out distracted, my head still spinning from whiskey and aftershocks of my orgasm as I dig my phone out of my tote. "Shit," I say again when I see the screen.

I look up to find him watching me. Max—was that his name?—breathing hard, his fly still undone.

His expression is a mix of uncertainty and something darker. Something helpless, and somehow almost demanding.

I wanted to linger. To sink back into the kiss. To let this moment stretch into something more.

But everyone was counting on me. Milo. Jessica. Kincade. I can't let myself get distracted by a stranger in a bar bathroom.

Especially not by the confusing pull of not wanting him to stay a stranger.

"Look..." I start, not sure what I'm even about to say.

For a dizzying second, I consider staying.

I could take this call, talk Kincade off whatever ledge he's on, then walk back to my place with Max. Finish this in an actual bed. Maybe grab coffee in the morning. Find out what made him have a bad year.

What am I doing?

I'm in a dive bar bathroom, not a Hallmark movie.

My phone buzzes again. I have to take this call, even though it's well past midnight. I need to stay focused on what matters.

This can't matter.

I need to leave. Alone.

"Look," I say, forcing a detached smile. "This was great. Really. Thank you." I lean up and press one last kiss to his mouth. "But I have to go."

I slip out of the bathroom and pull the door closed behind me, smoothing my skirt as I head for the exit.

"Close me out, Frankie!" I call over my shoulder. "Add twenty for you!"

"Okay, Harper," he answers with a wave. "See you next time."

I reach the front door and pause. Some reckless part of me hopes the handsome stranger will follow me.

He doesn't.

Good.

It's better this way.

At least that's what I tell myself as I step out into the cool midnight air.

Chapter 2

Max

I sit on my board and match my breathing to the steady rise and fall of the ocean, the horizon still pale with morning. My therapist's voice threads through my head, steady and annoying in the way things are when advice you didn't want to take is working.

Five things I can see: The sun just breaking over the water. The dark line of the shore. A gull skimming low across the surface. The scratches on the nose of my board. The slow rise of the swell beneath me.

Four things I can feel: The board under me. The cold seep of the Pacific through my wetsuit. The tight pull in my shoulders from paddling too frantically at first. The steady thump of my heart, slowing.

Three things I can hear: Water lapping against fiberglass. The distant crash of a wave breaking. My own breath, even and measured.

Two things I can smell: Salt air. Neoprene.

One thing I can taste: Her.

The faint memory of whiskey and her lips lingers longer than it has any right to.

And I didn't get enough.

Not that she owes me anything. She doesn't. The memory of her coming apart around my fingers could go to my grave with me as one of the best moments of my life. But it wasn't enough.

I wanted more.

I want it again—the sharp little gasp she made, the way those green eyes found mine when I touched her, the way her hand tightened in my hair, the brief sting as she pulled just hard enough. The way her body craved mine, leaning in, pulling closer. The way it convulsed when she finally let go.

And then her damn phone rang.

She didn't silence it.

Didn't ignore it.

Didn't toss it into the toilet the way I silently begged her to.

She answered it.

With my fingers still slick with her.

She slid off the counter, smoothed her skirt, and kissed me with the phone still pressed to her ear. And before I could process what was happening, before I could stop her, she was gone, disappearing out of the bathroom like maybe she did that all the time.

I didn't even get her name.

What was I thinking? I flew across the country to focus on work. Just work. To rebuild my career without losing myself this time.

This was supposed to be controlled. Safe. A test to see if I can dip my toe back in without letting it swallow me whole. To see if everything from the last year and a half actually stuck. The therapy, the affirmations, the slow work of figuring out how I broke and how to put myself back together.

Not to complicate things with a beautiful stranger who makes me want to break my own rules.

A set rolls in on the horizon, darker water lifting in a slow, deliberate line. I feel it before I really see it, the ocean drawing a breath. It's a good wave. Maybe more than one. The kind I would normally turn and paddle for without hesitation.

But I stay where I am, just beyond the break, letting it pass beneath me.

Since I started surfing again, this part has become as important as—maybe more than— catching the perfect wave. Learning patience. Learning that not every opportunity needs to be seized, not every swell chased. That disappointment doesn't mean failure.

That's what I'm supposed to be focused on. The steps of my recovery. Not letting old patterns dress themselves up as something new. Last night was impulsive. Exactly the kind of thing I'm supposed to avoid. I'm supposed to take three deep breaths before I say yes to anything.

But when she pressed her mouth to mine, or maybe when she tugged me into the bathroom, or hell, when she invited me to sit back down on the barstool, I knew I'd say yes to whatever she asked.

And that's the problem.

That's what got me here in the first place.

Why don't you feel like you can say no, Max? My therapist had asked during one of my first sessions—back when I was still bitter and angry and raw.

Because you don't get to the top by saying no.

You get there by being the one who always says yes.

The job. The marriage. Both required me to say yes to everything and no to myself. It worked—right up until it broke me.

I hold my fist up to the thin strip of sky between the horizon and the newly risen sun. 6 a.m.

I should head in. Shower. Get dressed.

Even if it's just a favor for an old friend.

Even if it's only three months.

Even if it's nowhere near the level of what I used to do.

Not every swell needs to be chased.

I turn my board toward shore, already feeling the familiar pull of routine settling back into place.

I should be on time for my first day at my new job. That's what matters.

Chapter 3

Harper

"You look like shit," Milo says, glancing up from the architectural renderings spread across the front table as I walk in.

I glance at my phone. Milo is never here before I am. But it's 8:07—I'm never this late. But I slept like shit, so no surprise I look like it too.

"Yeah, well, being told by your business partner that you can't do your job will do that to a girl." Saccharine sarcasm coating my voice as I drop my bag onto our office manager Jessica's desk.

"My guess is," Milo says, circling the table and waving a finger at me, "you exceeded your rule of no more than two top-shelf whiskeys, and put them all on the company credit card while cursing me, this job, and all of mankind."

"Not all of mankind," I reply. "The bartender at Bar None is cool."

Milo studies me long enough that I roll my shoulders back and stand a little taller.

We run a casual office—another way Milo and I promised ourselves we'd do things differently when we started Studio Mise—but today I wore heels. Power heels, my mom used to call them. At five-eight, I'm not short, but the extra height puts me eye to eye with Milo. And any idiot teenager I might have to deal with today.

"You know I don't think you're incapable, right?" Milo says, and I know him well enough to hear the careful way he chooses his words. "I think you care too much. You take on everyone's problems. You stay late so I can go home to Parker. You restructure deals to give Jessica a bigger cut. You take the blame when things go wrong, whether it's your fault or not."

I open my mouth to argue, but he holds up a hand.

"You give everyone else what they need, Harper. I wanted to hire someone to give you what you need."

"I'm fine, Milo."

"I know you think you are." He leans forward. "But this Bites by Blake concept is a big deal. It's exactly the exposure we've been looking for. I want it to go smoothly—"

"*I'll* make it go smoothly," I snap.

"Without it costing me my best friend," he continues evenly, "or her mental health."

"Next, you're going to try to make me meditate or some shit," I say, but I'm already softening.

"I wouldn't dream of it."

"So where did you find this kid anyway?" I glance around the front office like my new assistant might be hiding behind the curtains. "Am I going to have to put him down for a nap or drive him back for his seventh-period homeroom class?"

"Harper, he's not—"

"He better not ask me to fucking prom!" I say, disappearing into my office.

I drop into my desk chair and pull up the latest spreadsheets, but the numbers blur.

I try to focus on Kincade Smith's demands—the investor behind our next project. It was his idea to hand a restaurant to a viral TikToker—Blake Adams—on the assumption that we could capitalize on his millions of views. Instead, the chaos this project has unleashed is mind-numbing.

Kincade has a talent for harebrained demands disguised as brilliant ideas.

Like his call last night.

Last night.

The thought triggers a memory of my caramel-voiced bar companion. His hands on my body. His lips on my neck. The way his fingers coaxed me apart until I forgot, briefly, how tightly I hold myself together.

I'm no stranger to a well-placed one-night stand. But last night felt different. The orgasm was incredible, yes, but it was the ease of it, the connection, the way I caught myself imagining what came *after*, that has me off-balance eight hours later.

And maybe that's why I left in such a hurry.

Or that I'm wondering what he's doing right now. Where he might be.

I shake my head and click through to the budget tab.

Sure, if Kincade hadn't called rambling about something that absolutely could have waited until morning, I probably would have let Max fish a condom from his wallet and finish what we started. But it wasn't the interruption that rattled me.

It was the thought that I would have asked him to come home with me afterward.

Something I never do.

That thought unsettles me far more than anything Kincade was yammering about.

So I left. Without Max's number or any real way for either of us to find the other again. And honestly, it's probably better that way. For both of us.

I've more or less given up on men. Or at least on the idea that they can be anything more than a means to an end. I have good friends—Milo, Amelia, and Mr. Evans. And I have good sex when I have time for it. But I gave up on wanting both in the same person a long time ago. That's a recipe for disaster.

I'm married to my job. Just like my mom was.

I'm not naive; I saw where that got her. I always thought my dad was great, and I understand he was frustrated. Mom never put him before her work. But if he couldn't live with that, he should have had the decency to divorce her first before...before moving on.

That's why I keep my worlds separate.

Friends. Sex. Work.

Three distinct buckets. No messy overlap.

So whatever happened last night stays in that bathroom. One-time thing. Done. Over.

My phone pings.

Amelia: *Did you work all weekend or actually do something fun??*

I stare at the message from my best friend, unsure how to answer. I go for distraction instead.

Harper: *It was fine. How's my Penelope?*

Amelia: *Puking all weekend. I was hoping to live vicariously through you.*

I need to choose my words carefully. We tell each other everything, so too many or too few details and Amelia will know something's up. I'm not sure what to tell her, and I'm not ready to unpack that yet.

Harper: *You know, work, my favorite neighborhood dive bar, then more work*

I leave out the part about the hottest man I've ever met rendering me boneless in the bathroom.

I glance at the time. 8:45. Fifteen minutes until Sullivan Bennett arrives—assuming he's capable of getting himself out of bed before midmorning. Milo claims he told him nine, which is already a compromise. 9 a.m. is two hours later than I like to start my day, so my new assistant is already behind, and we haven't even met yet.

I hear Jessica talking animatedly to someone in the front office.

I round my desk, pausing inside my office door.

"You must be Sullivan?" she says in her perpetually too-perky lilt.

Here we go. Let's meet the toddler.

I straighten the belt of my intentionally all-black outfit and steel myself. I've learned it's best to let people assume I'm the villain right away. Milo can be the golden retriever. I'm the black cat.

"Oh, here's Ms. Wells now," Jessica chirps as I step out. "Harper, this is Sullivan."

"Benster!" Milo booms from his office down the hall.

"Harper?"

That voice—confused, warm, and unmistakably caramel-soft—stops me cold.

"Max?" I choke.

"No, Sullivan," Jessica corrects brightly.

"Benny, Ben, Benster," Milo continues, appearing behind us.

My head whips toward him.

"You're Harper?" Max asks again, pulling my attention back to his eyes. Those same amber pools I got lost in last night.

"Yes," Jessica says. "This is Harper Wells, your new boss."

My stomach drops.

"Benny, I'm so glad you're here," Milo sings, utterly oblivious to the emotional car crash unfolding in front of him.

"Why are you calling him *Benny*?" I snap, my irritation ricocheting in every direction at once.

"That's what we called him back in our Beta Kappa days."

"You were in a fraternity?" Jessica asks, delighted.

"Yeah," Milo shrugs. "Back when I was pretending to be straight."

"Why did you tell me your name was Max?" I demand, turning back to him.

"Wait—you've met?" Milo's eyes bounce between us like he's watching a tennis match.

"That's what I go by," Max says tightly. "Why didn't you tell me you were Harper?"

"I did."

"No, you didn't. Or I would have never—"

"Never what?" Milo asks.

"Nothing!" Max and I shout in perfect, horrifying unison.

The room goes silent. My heart hammers so loudly I'm sure everyone can hear it.

"Okay," Jessica says after a beat, glancing down at her clipboard. "So you go by Max?"

"Yeah. It's my middle name." He doesn't take his glare off me.

Sullivan M. Bennett.

"It's on my résumé," he adds, clipped. And it's clearly directed at me.

"Oh! You're right." Jessica nods, scribbling. "Preferred name: Max. Not a problem. All your forms still have your full legal name."

"What kind of name is Sullivan?" I quip, not entirely sure why.

"You didn't seem concerned about my name last night," he says—low enough that only I hear.

"Okay!" Milo says, his eyes flicking warily between us. "Sullivan Maxwell Bennett, this is my business partner, Harper Eloise Wells. I don't have a middle name, but I like to pretend it's Prince."

"Could you sign here, Sull—Max," Jessica says, thrusting the clipboard at him.

He takes it without breaking eye contact with me. His jaw is tight, a muscle ticking beneath his cheekbone.

And while I'm not one to back down from confrontation, I suddenly have somewhere I need to be. Anywhere but here. I don't need an assistant. And I definitely don't need one whose hands were on my—

"I need to go," I snap, grabbing my bag. "Jessica will—" What? Show him around? Set up a desk for him in my office so I have to sit five feet from him and somehow ignore the way his voice does unforgettable things to my insides? I can't think. "Milo will get you settled out here."

And then I walk out of the office.

I'm not sure where I'm going.

Only that I cannot stay here.

Acknowledgements

Since the list of people who helped bring this book into the world hasn't changed since *Faking It* (Jen, Meg, Mary, Brooke, Amy, my parents, and my husband—you are still my constants), I wanted to take a moment to thank someone else just as important: **you**.

The incredible indie romance community—readers and writers alike—deserves its own special shout-out.

Because of you, millions of aspiring authors like me get the chance to share our hearts with the world. You give us permission to step out of the chaos for a minute and escape into a simpler, happier, and let's be honest...far spicier world.

Romance readers make up one of the most passionate and devoted corners of publishing, accounting for a huge share of all books sold each year. Your enthusiasm, your reviews, your endless TBR stacks—you're the reason this whole ecosystem thrives.

Writing these stories has brought so much joy, purpose, and downright fun into my life. So to you, dear reader, and to my fellow writers hustling and dreaming right alongside me, thank you for making all of this possible.

About the Author

AJ Claremont writes contemporary romance packed with flirty banter, swoony heroes, and enough spice to make you fan yourself while you read.

Her stories are full of women who are both fearless and flawed, and men who are devoted but delightfully complicated — because the best love stories are never simple.

Fueled by coffee, 90s hip hop, and an endless imagination, AJ lives in Northern California with her real-life swoony husband, their two awesome teenagers, and an ever-growing TBR stack.

Keep up with AJ at ajclaremont.com or @ajclaremontwrites on Instagram

www.ingramcontent.com/pod-product-compliance
Lightning Source LLC
La Vergne TN
LVHW090611110826
845146LV00001B/342

* 9 7 9 8 9 8 5 1 0 8 2 4 8 *